Nan Of The Gypsies

Grace May North

Copyright © 2023 Culturea Editions
Text and cover : © public domain
Edition : Culturea (Hérault, 34)
Contact : infos@culturea.fr
Print in Germany by Books on Demand
Design and layout : Derek Murphy
Layout : Reedsy (https://reedsy.com/)
ISBN : 9791041849314
Légal deposit : August 2023
All rights reserved

NAN OF THE GYPSIES

CHAPTER I.

GYPSY NAN.

One glorious autumn day, when the pale mellow gold of the sunshine softened the ruggedness of the encircling mountains and lay caressingly on the gnarled live oaks, on the sky-reaching eucalyptus, and on the red-berried pepper trees, a tinkling of bells was heard on the long highway that led into the little garden village of San Seritos, half asleep by the gleaming blue Pacific. A gypsy caravan, consisting of three covered wagons drawn by teams of six mules, and followed by a string of horses, drew to one side of the road and stopped. A band of nut-brown, fox-like children scrambled down and began to race about, the older ones gathering sticks for the camp fire which they knew would soon be needed.

Four men, aquiline nosed, and with black hair hanging in ringlets to their shoulders, and as many women, gaudily dressed, with red and yellow silk handkerchiefs wound about their heads, prepared to make camp for the night.

It was a fittingly picturesque spot for a clump of gnarled live oaks grew about a spring of clear, cold water, which, fed from some hidden source, was never dry.

A quarter of a mile away lay the first of the beautiful estates and homes of Spanish architecture, for which San Seritos was far famed.

One of the gypsy women paused at her task to shade her eyes and gaze back over the highway as though expecting someone.

A mis-shapen goblin-like boy tugged on her sleeve, and with a wistful expression in his dark eyes, he whispered, "Manna Lou, Nan hasn't run away again, has she?"

"I don' no," the gypsy answered, drearily. "Maybe yes and maybe not."

A moment later, when the woman had returned to her task, there was a screaming of delight among the fox-like children, and Tirol, the mis-shapen boy, cried in a thrill glad voice, "Here she comes, Manna Lou! Here comes Gypsy Nan."

Toward them down the mountain drive, galloping on a spirited mottled pony, rode a beautiful young girl of thirteen, her long black hair, straight to her shoulders, suddenly broke into a riot of ringlets and hung to her waist. Her gown and headdress were as bright as maple leaves in Autumn, and her dark brown eyes were laughing with merriment and mischief.

As she sprang from her pony, the gypsy children leaped upon her, uttering animal-like cries of joy, but Tirol, hobbling to her side, caught her warm brown hand in his thin claw-like one and looked up at her with adoration in his hungering black eyes as he said: "I was 'fraid, Sister Nan, 'fraid you had gone again, and maybe this time for good."

The gypsy girl knelt impulsively and caught the mis-shapen boy in her arms, and her eyes flashed as she said passionately: "Little Tirol, Nan will never, never go for good as long as you need her to protect you from that wicked Anselo Spico. I hate him, hate him, because he abuses a poor boy who can't grow strong and defend himself, but he won't strike you again, little Tirol, unless he strikes me first."

"Hush!" warningly whispered Cyra, a small gypsy girl. "Here comes Spico. He's been ahead to look over the village."

It was evident by the suspending work in the camp that the approaching horseman was someone of importance in their midst. A Romany rye was he, dressed in blue corduroy with a scarlet sash at his waist and a soft scarlet ribbon knotted about his broad brimmed felt hat.

His dark, handsome face, which, when in repose had an expression of either vanity or cruelty, was smiling as he dismounted from his spirited black horse.

Gypsy Nan, who had been standing in the shadow of a live oak with protecting arms about the goblin-like Tirol breathed a sigh of relief, for the hated Spico was evidently in the best of spirits. He called gayly after the tall gypsy lad who was leading his horse away: "Soobli, where is Mizella, your queen? Call her forth, I have good news to tell."

3

While he was talking the curtains of the largest van were pushed apart, an old hag-like gypsy appeared, and, with much groaning, made her way down the wooden steps to the ground. There she leaned heavily on a cane, and hobbling toward her son, asked eagerly: "What's the pickings like to be, Spico? Is it a rich gorigo town?"

"Rich, Mother Mizella?" the handsome young rye repeated. "The gorigo around here has his pockets lined with gold and will spend it freely if he is amused. You women dress in your gayest and start out tomorrow with your tambourines. You will gather in much money with your fortune telling and we men in the village will not be idle."

Then, going to the camp fire, over which a small pig was being roasted, he asked, looking around sharply. "Where is leicheen Nan? If she has run away again, I'll—"

"No, no, Nan hasn't run away," the gypsy woman, Manna Lou, hastened to say. "She's here, Spico. Come Nan, dearie," she called pleadingly. "Come and speak pleasant."

The girl, with a defiant flashing of her dark eyes, stepped out of the shadow of a low-branching live oak and stood in the full light of the camp fire.

"Leicheen Nan," the Romany rye said, and his words were a command, "tomorrow you will go to the village and dance at the gorigo inn. You have idled long enough."

It was the gypsy woman, Manna Lou, who replied. "Not yet, Spico," she implored in a wheedling tone—"Nan is only a little gothlin. Wait until she is grown."

Before the angered young rye could answer, Mizella hobbled to the camp fire and snarled angrily: "I am queen. My word is law. That good-for-nothing leicheen Nan shall do as my son says."

The girl stepped back into the shadow, her heart rebellious. She said nothing, but she was determined that she would not obey.

The men then sat about the fire and were served by the women, who, with the children afterwards ate what was left.

The moon came up, and Nan, nymph-like, danced up a grassy hill back of the camp. A throng of wild, fox-like little children scrambled up after her. "A story. Tell us a story, Nanny," they called. The girl paused, turned and seeing the crippled Tirol struggling to climb the hill, she ran back, lifted him to her strong young shoulder and carried him to the top of the knoll. There they all sat together, many bright black eyes watching while Nan told them a story. A fanciful tale it was of how a gypsy princess had been cruelly treated by a wicked man like Anselo Spico. How he had shut the princess and six other gypsy girls, who had defied him, in a van without horses and had let it roll down a cliff road into the sea. "But they were not drowned, for the spirits of the sea-spray carried them up to the sky, and any clear night you can see that gypsy princess and the six gypsy girls dancing in their bright crimson and gold shawls and you call it the sunset."

Tirol, always the most intense of Nan's listeners leaned forward and asked in a low whisper: "What did the sea-spray spirits do to—to that wicked Romany rye?"

"That night," the gypsy girl said in a low voice of mystery, "he went to the top of a cliff to make sure the van had gone into the sea, and it had, for it lay broken in the surf. Then the sea-spray spirits lifted a wave as high as a hill and it swept over the cliff and that wicked Romany rye was seen no more."

Tirol's black eyes glowed in the moonlight and his frail hand was trembling as Nan took it to lift him again to her shoulder.

"Steal back soft-like, so he won't know we left camp," she warned. Crouching low, the file of little fox-like children crept back of trees and brush until the vans were reached, then darted between the flaps and crawled, without undressing, into their bunk-like beds, all but Nan and Tirol. The gypsy girl felt smothered if she slept in the van.

5

CHAPTER II.

THE GARDEN-ALL-AGLOW.

Before day break, Gypsy Nan awakened the goblin-like boy. Rolled in blankets they had slept in the shelter of the live oak trees and close to the warm coals of the camp fire.

"Come Tirol," she whispered, glancing at the wagons, to see if anyone was astir, "we must go now, for Nan isn't going to dance at the inn for the gorigo. And you must come, too, else that wicked Anselo Spico will make you stand on a corner and beg, making money out of your poor little bent body that's always a-hurting you."

With many backward glances the two children stole away to where the mules and ponies were corralled. After carefully lifting the frail boy to the back of the mottled horse, Binnie, Nan mounted, and together they galloped down the coast highway. The last star had faded, the grey in the East was brightening, and then suddenly the sun, in a burst of glory appeared and the sky and sea flamed rose and amethyst. The dark eyes of the girl glowed with appreciation and joy, and she started singing a wild, glad song to a melody of her own creating.

They had gone perhaps a mile from camp and away from the town when Nan suddenly drew rein and listened. She heard the beating of hoofs behind them, but the riders were hidden by the curve in the road.

Whirling her pony's head she turned down into a canyon that led to the shore. There she concealed her horse and with Tirol she lay close to the sand.

Two horsemen passed on the highway, and, as she had surmised, one was Anselo Spico. She thought they were hunting for her but she was mistaken. In the village the Romany rye had heard of a rich gorigo whose horses were of the finest breed and whose stables were but slightly guarded, and it was to inspect this place that they were going.

True, Mizella's son had noticed Nan's absence that morning but he knew that she would return and he was planning a cruel punishment which he would administer for her defiance and disobedience.

Nan remained in hiding until she could no longer hear the beating of the hoofs, then she said gaily—"Look Tirol, the sand is hard on the beach. I'll lift you up again, dearie, and we'll ride along by the sea."

The boy laughed happily as they rode, so close to the waves that now and then one broke about the pony's feet, and the girl laughed, too, for it is easy to forget troubles when one is young.

They soon came to a beautiful estate where the park-like grounds reached the edge of the gleaming white sand, but it was surrounded by a hedge so high that even on the small horse's back the children could not see over it.

"Tirol," Nan exclaimed, "no one could find us here, and so close up to this high hedge, we'll have our breakfast."

Leaping from the pony the girl, with tender compassion, carefully lifted down the mis-shapen boy, then opening a bundle tied in a red handkerchief, she gave him a thick slice of brown bread and a piece of roasted pig, which she had stored away the evening before.

"Look! Look!" cried the boy, clapping his claw-like hands. "The birds are begging, Nanny, let Tirol feed them."

Like a white cloud shining in the sun the sea gulls winged down from the sky. Gypsy Nan leaped to her feet and ran with outstretched arms to greet them, and the white birds fearlessly circled about her as she tossed crumbs into the air, and one, braver than the others lighted on Tirol's outstretched hand and pecked at his breakfast.

When at last this merry feast was over, the sea gulls flew away, and Nan called merrily, "Tirol, maybe there's something beautiful behind the hedge that's so high. Let's go through it, shall we?"

The deformed boy nodded. Many an exciting adventure he and Nan had when they ran away. But the gypsy children found that the hedge was as dense as it was high, and though it was glowing with small crimson flowers, it was also bristling with thorns and nowhere was there space enough for them to break through.

Suddenly Nan, who had danced ahead, gave a little cry of delight. "Here's the gate, Tirol!" she called. "It opens on the beach."

Eagerly the girl lifted the latch and to her joy the gate swung open. She leaped within and the boy followed her. Then for one breathless moment Gypsy Nan stood with clasped hands and eyes aglow, as she gazed about her.

Never before had she seen so wonderful a garden. There were masses of crysanthemums, golden in the sunlight, and, too, there were banks of flaming scarlet. In the midst of it all, glistening white in the sunshine, was a group of marble nymphs, evidently having a joyous time sporting in the fern-encircled pool, while a flashing of rainbow colors showered about them from the fountain. A mockingbird sang in the pepper tree near the house but there was no other sound.

"Let's find the gorigo lady that lives here," Nan whispered. "Maybe she'd let me tell her fortune. Anselo Spico won't be so angry if we take back a silver dollar."

Up the flowered path, the gypsy children went, but, though Nan fearlessly lifted the heavy wrought iron knocker on the door nearest the garden and on the one at the side, there was no response.

Returning to the garden, the girl stooped and passionately kissed a glowing yellow crysanthemum.

"Nan loves you! Nan loves you bright, beautiful flower!" she said in a low tense voice, "Nan would like to keep you."

"If you're wantin' it, why don't you take it?" t Tirol asked. "Spico an' the rest, they always take what they want when they can get it easy."

The girl turned upon the small boy as she said almost fiercely. "Haven't I told you time and again that 'tisn't honest to steal? Don't matter who does it, 'tisn't right, Tirol. Manna Lou said my mother wouldn't love me if I stole or lied. An' I won't steal! I won't lie! I won't."

Many a time Nan had been well beaten because she would not do these things which so often Anselo Spico had commanded.

Then, noting how the small boy shrank away as if frightened, the girl knelt and held him close in a passionate embrace. "Tirol!" she implored, "Little Tirol, don't be scared of Nan. 'Twasn't you she was fierce at. 'Twas him as makes every-body and all the little ones lie and steal. All the little ones that don't dare not because he would beat them."

The girl felt Tirol's frail body trembling in her clasp. "There, there, dearie. You needn't be afraid. Anselo Spico don't dareto beat you. He knows if he did, I'd kill him."

Then there was one of the changes of mood that were so frequently with Nan. Kissing Tirol, she danced away, flinging her body in wild graceful movements. Up one path she went, and down another. Catching up the tambourine which always hung at her belt, she shook it, singing snatches of song until she was quite tired out. Then, sinking down on a marble bench, she held Tirol close and gazed up at the windows of the house. One after another she scanned but no face appeared.

Had the proud, haughty owner of that house been at home, she would have felt that her grounds were being polluted by the presence of a gypsy.

Suddenly Nan sprang up and held out her hand for the frail claw-like one of the mis-shapen boy.

"No need to wait any longer. There's no lady here to get a dollar from for telling her fortune,—an' I'm glad, glad! Fortunes are just lies! I hate telling fortunes!"

Down the path they went toward the little gate in the high hedge which opened out upon the beach. Turning, before she closed it, the girl waved her free hand and called joyfully. "Good-bye flowers of gold, Nan's coming back some day."

CHAPTER III.

GOOD-BYE LITTLE TIROL.

The gypsy children returned toward the camp just as the sun was setting. "Aren't you 'fraid that Spico'll strike us?" the goblin-like boy asked, holding close to Nan as the small, mottled pony galloped along the coast road.

"No; I'm not scared," Nan said. "If he strikes us, we'll run away for good."

"Could we go back and live in that garden?"

"I don't know where we'd go. Somewheres! Maybe up there." Nan pointed and the boy glanced at the encircling mountains where the canyons were darkening. Surely they would be well hidden there. They were close enough now to see the smoke curling up from the camp fire near the clump of live oaks.

Leaving the small horse in the rope corral with the others, the children approached the wagons, keeping hidden behind bushes as best they could. Nan wanted to see who was about the fire before she made her presence known. The one whom she dreaded was not there and so she boldly walked into the circle of the light, leading Tirol. Then she spoke the gypsies' word of greeting: "Sarishan, Manna Lou."

"Leicheen Nan, dearie, how troubled my heart has been about you," the gypsy woman said. "You ran away. I thought forever."

"Where is Anselo Spico?" the girl inquired.

"He hasn't come yet. Mizella's been asking this hour back. He said at high sun he'd be here sure, more than likely he's been—"

"Hark!" Nan whispered, putting a protecting arm about the boy. "Hide, quick, Tirol, here he comes."

But only one horseman appeared, galloping through the dusk, and that one was Vestor, who had ridden away with the Romany rye that morning. His dark face told them nothing and yet they knew that he had much to tell. They gathered about him, but before he could speak, the old queen pushed her way to the front. "Where's my son?" she demanded.

"In jail for tryin' to steal a rich gorigo's horse." Then Vestor added mysteriously. "But he'll join us afore dawn, I'm tellin' you! Break camp at once," he commanded. "We're to wait for Spico in a mountain canyon on t'other side of town. I know where 'tis. I'll ride the leader."

The supper was hastily eaten, the fire beaten out, the mules and horses watered and hitched. Just as the moon rose over the sea, the gypsy caravan began moving slowly down the coast highway.

Nan, riding on her mottled pony, sincerely wished that Anselo Spico would not escape, but he always did, as she knew only too well.

Two hours later the caravan stopped on a lonely mountain road and drew to one side. Half an hour later everyone was asleep, but in the middle of the night Nan was awakened by a familiar voice.

Anselo Spico had returned.

Long before daybreak the gypsy caravan was once more under way. The jolting of the wagon of Manna Lou roused the girl. She climbed from her berth and looked in the one lower to see if all was well with little Tirol. Two big black eyes gazed out at her and one of the claw-like hands reached toward her. Nan took it lovingly.

"Little Tirol," she said, "you aren't feeling well." The goblin-like boy shook his head as he replied: "A crooked back hurts, Sister Nan. It hurts all the time."

"I know—I know dearie!" the girl said tenderly gathering the little fellow close in her arms. "Wait, Nan will bring you some breakfast." But the boy turned away and wearily closed his eyes.

The caravan had stopped long enough to make a fire and prepare the morning coffee. Soon Manna Lou entered the wagon. "Go out, Nan darling," she said. "Don't fear Spico. He only thinks of getting across the border in safety."

The girl beckoned to the gypsy woman and said in a low voice, "Little Tirol's not so well. We'd ought to stop at the next town and fetch a doctor."

"Poor little Tirol," the gypsy woman said kindly. "You'll be lonely, Nan, to have him go, but if the gorigo is right, if there is a heaven, then little Tirol'll be happier, for there's been no harm in him here. And there can't be anyone so cruel as Anselo Spico's been."

Nan clenched her hands and frowned. Manna Lou continued. "Perhaps his own mother Zitha will be there waiting, and she'll take care of him. Before she died, she gave me little Tirol and begged me to keep watch over him and I've done my best."

Impulsively Nan put her arms about the gypsy woman as she said, "Manna Lou, how good, how kind you are! You've been just like a mother to little Tirol and me, too. Some day you're going to tell me who my own mother was, aren't you, Manna Lou?"

"Yes, leicheen Nan. When you're eighteen, then I'm going to tell you. I promised faithful I wouldn't tell before that."

As the morning wore on, it was plain to the watchers that little Tirol was very ill and when at noon the caravan stopped, Nan, leaping from the wagon of Manna Lou confronted Anselo Spico as she said courageously: "Little Tirol is like to die. We've got to stop at that town down there into the valley and fetch a doctor."

"Got to?" sneered the dark handsome man, then he smiled wickedly. "Since when is leicheen Nan the queen of this tribe that she gives commands? What we've got to do is cross over the border into Mexico before the gorigo police gets track of us."

He turned away and Nan with indignation and pity in her heart, went back to the wagon. As she sat by the berth, holding Tirol's hot hand, she determined that as soon as the village was reached she herself would ride ahead and find a doctor.

Manna Lou had tried all of the herbs, but nothing of which the gypsies knew could help the goblin-like boy or quiet his cruel pain.

It was mid-afternoon when Nan saw that the winding downward road was leading into a valley town. It would take the slow moving caravan at least an hour to reach the village, while Nan, on her pony, could gallop there very quickly. Not far below was a dense grouping of live oak trees. She would slip among them on Binnie and then, out of sight of the caravan, she would gallop across the fields to the town. "Manna Lou," the girl said softly that she need not awaken the sleeping Tirol, "I'm going for a little ride."

"That's nice, dearie," the kind gypsy woman replied. "It will do you good. The sunshine is warm and cheery."

It was a rough road and the caravan was moving slowly. Many of the fox-like gypsy children were running alongside, and Nan joined them.

She wanted to be sure where Anselo Spico was riding. As she had hoped, he was on the driver's seat of Queen Mizella's wagon which was always in the lead.

Running back, she was about to mount her pony when she heard her name called softly. Turning, she saw Manna Lou beckoning to her. Springing to the home wagon, she went inside.

"What is it, Manna Lou?" she asked. "You look so strange."

"We thought little Tirol was asleep all this time, and so hewas, but it's the kind of sleep that you don't waken from. Maybe he's in the gorigo heaven now with Zitha, his mother."

The girl felt awed. "Why, Manna Lou," she whispered, "little Tirol looks happier than I ever saw him before. See how sweetly he's smiling."

"Yes, dearie, he is happier, for his poor, crooked back was always hurting him, but he was a brave little fellow, cheerful and uncomplaining."

The caravan stopped and Manna Lou went out to tell the others what had happened. The gypsy girl, alone with the boy who had so loved her, knelt by his side and kissing him tenderly, she said: "Little Tirol, darling, Nan has staid here and put up with the cruelty of Angelo Spico, just to be taking care of you, but now that you aren't needing Nan any more, she's going far away. Good-bye, dearie."

* * * * * * * *

That night while the caravan was moving at a slow pace over the moonlit road and all save the drivers were asleep, Nan, slipped out of Manna Lou's wagon, leaped to the back of Binnie and galloped back by the way they had come.

CHAPTER IV.

NAN ESCAPES.

All night long Gypsy Nan, on the back of her small horse Binnie climbed the steep mountain road, a full moon far over her head transforming everything about her to shimmering silver.

A bundle tied in a beautiful shawl of scarlet and gold contained all that belonged to her and food enough to last for several days.

Nan was on the ridge of a mountain road when the sun rose, and to her joy saw the village of San Seritos lying in the valley below, and beyond was the gleaming blue sea.

She drew rein and gazed ahead wondering where she should go, when her ears, trained to notice all of nature's sounds, heard the startled cry of some little ground animal. Dismounting, she bent over the place from which the sound had come and saw an evil-eyed rattle-snake about to spring upon a squirrel that seemed powerless to get away.

Nan, whose heart was always filled with pity for creatures that were weak and helpless, threw a rock at the snake which glided into the underbrush. Then she lifted the squirrel, feeling its heart pounding against her hand. She carried the little thing across the road and placed it on an overhanging limb of a live oak tree.

"There now! Nan's given you a chance to get away from the snake. That's what Anselo Spico is, a rattle-snake, an' I'm trying to get away."

She was about to mount on her pony when she again paused and listened intently. This time she heard the galloping of a horse. Peering through the trees, back of her, she saw a black pony and its rider fairly plunging down the rough road on the opposite side of the canyon she had just crossed. In half an hour, perhaps less, that horse and rider would reach the spot where she was standing.

Nan's fears were realized. She was being pursued. The rider she knew even at that distance, to be Vestor, a cruel man who would do anything his master Anselo Spico commanded.

Where could she hide? It would have been easier if she had been alone, but it would not be a simple matter to conceal the pony. Mounting, the girl raced ahead. A turn in the mountain road brought her to a ranch. It was so very early that no one was astir. Riding in and trusting to fate to protect her, she went at once to a great barn and seeing a stack of hay in one corner, she wedged her pony back of it and stood, scarcely breathing, waiting for, she knew not what, to happen.

But, although the moments dragged into an hour, no one came. At last, unable to endure the suspense longer, the girl slipped from her hiding-place, and, keeping close to the wall of the old barn she sidled slowly toward a wide door. She heard voices not far away.

"You ain't seen nothing of a black-haired wench in a yellar an' red dress?"

It was Vestor speaking and it was quite evident that he was snarling angry. Nan peered through a knot-hole, her heart beating tempestuously. The gypsy's gimlet-like black eyes were keeping a sharp lookout all about him as he talked. The rancher's back was toward the girl. He, at first, quietly replied, but when Vestor took a step toward the barn, saying he'd take a look around himself, the brawny rancher caught his arm, whirled him about and pointed toward the road. "I'll have none of your kind prowlin' about my place. You'd lake a look, all right, but I reckon you'd take everything else that wa'n't held down wi' a ton of rock.

"I know the thievin', lying lot of you. I'd as soon shoot one of you down as I would a skunk, an' sooner, if 'twant for the law upholding of you, though gosh knows why it does." Then, as Vestor kept looking intently at the open barn door, the rancher, infuriated by the man's doggedly remaining when he had been told to be off, sprang toward a wagon, snatched a whip and began to lash the gypsy about the legs.

With cries of pain, Vestor turned an ugly visage toward the rancher, but meeting only determination and equal hatred, he thought better of his attempt to spring at him, turned, went to his black pony, mounted it and rode rapidly back the way he had come.

He didn't want to be too far behind the caravan fearing that the gorigo police might take him up and put him in jail on Anselo's offense.

The rancher stood perfectly still for sometime after the gypsy had ridden away, then he also turned and looked toward the barn. Nan had at once sidled to her place back of the hay stack and so she did not see that he slowly walked that way.

Stopping in the door he listened intently. Then shrugging his shoulders, he went into the house to his breakfast. Half an hour later he again sauntered to the barn door. "Gal," he called. "Hi, there, you gypsy gal! That black soul'd critter's gone this long while. Don't be afeard to come out. Ma's waitin' to give you some breakfast."

Surely Nan could trust a voice so kindly. Timidly she appeared, leading the pony who was munching a mouthful of hay. The rancher smiled at the girl in a way to set her fears at rest, at least as far as he was concerned, but once out in the open she glanced around wildly. — "Where is he? Where's that Vestor gone? Will he be back?"

For answer, the rancher motioned the girl to follow him. He led her to a high peak back of the barn. "You kin see from here to all sides," he said: "You lie low, sort of, behind that big rock an' keep watchin'. The scoundrel rode off that a-way. If he keep's a goin', you'll see him soon. If he turned back, well, I'll let out the dogs." Nan did as she had been told and from that high position, she soon saw, far across the canyon, riding rapidly to the south, the black pony bearing the man she feared.

She rose greatly relieved. "He's gone sure enough, Vestor has." Then, suspiciously she turned toward the man. "How did you know where I was?"

"I saw you go in," the rancher told her, "an' I was settin' outside waitin for you to come out with whatever 'twas, you'd gone in to steal."

A dark red mantled the girl's face, and she said in a low voice. "I don't steal an' I don't lie, but he does." She jerked her head in the direction Vestor had taken. "So do the rest, mostly, but, they don't all. Manna Lou don't steal and she don't lie. She fetched me up not to."

17

The girl's dark eyes looked into the penetrating grey eyes of the rancher with such a direct gaze that he believed her.

A woman appeared on the back porch and called to them. "Fetch the gal in for a bite of breakfast if she ain't too wild like."

"Thanks, but I don't want any breakfast," Nan said. Then, noting that Binnie was still chewing on the hay he had pulled from the stack, she added, —"I haven't any money, or I'd pay for what he's had. I couldn't keep him from eating it."

"Of course you couldn't, gal," the rancher said kindly. Then, as he saw that the girl was determined to mount her pony and ride away, he asked — "Where are you going to? I don't have to ask what you're running away from? I know that purty well."

The girl shook her head and without a smile, she again said "Thanks." Then, quite unexpectedly, for the man had seen her make no sign, the pony broke into a run and she was gone.

CHAPTER V.

NAN REVISITS THE GARDEN.

For half an hour Nan rode, bent low in her saddle possibly with the thought that she would be less noticeable. Each time that the winding road brought her to an open place where she could see across the valley, she drew rein and gazed steadily at the ribbon-like trail which appeared, was lost to sight, and re-appeared for many miles to the south.

At last what she sought was seen, a horseman so small because of the distance that he appeared no larger than a toy going rapidly away. Sitting erect, the girl gazed down in the other direction and saw the garden city of San Seritos between the mountains and the sea.

"Ho, Binnie!" she cried, her black eyes glowing. "I know where we'll go. — Back to that beach place where the flowers of gold are."

And then, in the glory of the still early morning, with her black hair flying back of her, the girl in the red and yellow dress galloped down to the highway and rode around the village, that no-one might see her and arrest her because she was a gypsy.

There were but few astir at so early an hour, but the sun was high in the heavens when at last she reached the little ravine that led down to the sea.

This time she breakfasted alone in the shadow of the high hedge, and the shining white birds did not come.

"Perhaps they only came for little Tirol," she thought. Then springing up, she stretched her arms toward the gleaming blue sky as she said: "I do want little Tirol to be happy."

This was an impulse and not a prayer, for the gypsies had no religion, and Nan knew nothing really of the heaven of the gorigo.

Then, telling Binnie to wait for her she opened the gate and entered the garden. The masses of golden and scarlet bloom, the glistening of many colors in the fountain, the joyous song of birds in the red-berried pepper trees fascinated the gypsy girl, and she danced about like some wild thing, up and down the garden paths, pausing now and then to press her cheek passionately against a big yellow crysanthemum that stood nearly as tall as she, and to it she would murmur lovingly in strange Romany words.

She was following a path which she and Tirol had not found, suddenly she paused and listened. She had heard voices, and peering through the low hanging branches of an ornamental tree, she saw a pretty cottage by the side of great iron gates that stood ajar. Here lived the head gardener and his little family. A buxum, kindly faced young woman was talking to a small girl of seven.

"Now, Bertha, watch Bobbie careful," she was saying. "Mammy is going up to the big house. The grand ladies is comin' home today an' every-thin' must be spic and ready."

Nan darted deeper among the shrubs and bushes for the young woman passed so close that she could have touched her. The gypsy girl remained in hiding and watched the small children who looked strange to her with their flaxen hair and pink cheeks used as she was to the dark-eyed, black-haired, fox-like little gypsies.

The baby boy was a chubby laughing two-year-old, "Birdie," as he called his sister, played with him for a time on the grass in front of their cottage. At last, wearying of this, she said—"Now Bobby, you sit right still like a mouse while Birdie goes and fetches out her dollie."

Springing up, the little girl ran indoors. A second later a butterfly darted past the wee boy. Gurgling in delight, he scrambled to his feet and toddled uncertainly after it. Out through the partly-open iron gates he went, and then, tripping, he sprawled in the dust of the roadway. At that same instant Nan heard the chugging of an oncoming machine and leaping from her hiding place, she darted through the gates and into the road. A big touring car was swerving around a corner. The frightened baby, after trying to scramble to his feet, had fallen again.

Nan, seizing him, hurled him to the soft grass by the roadside. Then she fell and the machine passed over her. The "grand ladies" had returned.

The car stopped almost instantly, and the chauffeur lifted the limp form of the gypsy girl in his arms.

"I don't think she's dead, Miss Barrington," he said, "and if you ladies wish I'll take her right to the county hospital as quickly as I can."

The older woman spoke coldly. "No, I would not consider that I was doing my duty if I sent her to the county hospital. You may carry her into the house, Martin, and then procure a physician at once."

"But, Miss Barrington, she's nothing but a gypsy, and yours the proudest family in all San Seritos or anywhere for that," the man said, with the freedom of an old servant.

Then, it was that the other lady spoke, and in her voice was the warmth of pity and compassion.

"Of course we'll take the poor child into our home," she said. "She may be only a gypsy girl, but no greater thing can anyone do than risk his own life for another."

And so the seemingly lifeless Gypsy Nan was carried into the mansion-like home which stood in the garden-all-aglow that she had so loved.

CHAPTER VI.

ONLY A GYPSY-GIRL.

When at last the girl opened her eyes, she looked about her in half dazed wonder. Where could she be? In a room so beautiful that she thought perhaps it was the gorigo heaven. The walls were the blue of the sky, and the draperies were the gold of the sun, while the wide windows framed glowing pictures of the sea and the garden.

For the first time in her roaming life, Nan was in a luxurious bed. Hearing the faint rustle of leaves at her side, she turned her head and saw a grey-haired, kindly faced woman, who was gowned in a soft silvery cashmere; a bow of pink fastened the creamy lace mantle about her shoulders. It was Miss Dahlia Barrington, who was reading a large book. Hearing a movement from the bed, she looked up with a loving smile, and closing the book, she placed it on a table and bent over the wondering eyed girl.

"Where am I, lady?" Nan asked.

"You are in the Barrington Manor, dear. My sister's home and mine. Do you not recall what happened?"

"Yes, lady, was the little boy hurt, lady?"

"Indeed not, thanks to you," Miss Dahlia said. "Tell me your name, dear, that I may know what to call you."

The girl's dark eyes grew wistful and she looked for a moment out toward the sea. Then she said in a very low voice. "I don't know my name, only just Nan." It was then she remembered that her race was scorned by the white gorigo, and, trying to rise, she added, "I must go now, lady. I must go back to Manna Lou. I'm only a gypsy. You won't want me here."

"Only a gypsy?" the little woman said gently, as she covered the brown hand lovingly with her own frail white one. "Dearie, you are just as much a child of God as I am or Miss Barrington is, or indeed, any-one."

Nan could not understand the words, for they were strange to her, but she could understand the loving caress, and, being weary, she again closed her eyes, but a few moments later she was aroused by a cold, unloving voice that was saying: "Yes, doctor, I understand that she is a gypsy, and that probably she will steal everything that she can lay her hands on, but I will have things locked up when she is strong enough to be about. I consider that she was sent here by Providence, and that it is therefore my duty to keep the little heathen and try to civilize and Christianize her."

It was the older Miss Barrington who was speaking. Nan, who had never stolen even a flower, was keenly hurt, and she determined to run away as soon as ever she could.

The chimes of the great clock in the lower hall were musically telling the midnight hour when the girl, seemingly strengthened by her determined resolve, sat up in bed and listened intently.

She had heard a noise beyond the garden hedge, and her heart leaped joyously. It was Binnie, her mottled pony, calling to her. All day long he had been waiting for her.

"I'm coming, Binnie darling," the gypsy girl whispered. Then, climbing from the bed, she dressed quickly, and, fearing that if she opened the door she might be heard, she climbed through the window and on a vine covered trellis descended to the garden.

How beautiful it was in the moonlight, she thought, but she dared not pause. Down the path she sped and out at the gate in the hedge.

Binnie, overjoyed at seeing his mistress, whinnied again.

Gypsy Nan gave the small horse an impulsive hug as she whispered: "Binnie dearie, be quiet or some one will hear you. We must go away now, far, far away."

The pony, seemingly to understand, trotted along on the hard sand with the gypsy girl clinging to his back, for the strength, which had seemed to come to her when she determined to run away, was gone and she felt weak and dazed. A few moments later she slipped from the pony's back and lay unconscious on the sand while the faithful Binnie stood guard over her.

It was not until the next afternoon that she again opened her eyes and found herself once more in the beautiful blue and gold room and at her bedside sat the gentle Miss Dahlia gazing at her with an expression of mingled sorrow and loving tenderness.

"Little Nan," she said, when she saw that the girl had awakened, "Why did you run away from me?"

"Not from you, lady, from the other one, who called me thief."

Miss Dahlia glanced quickly toward the door as she said softly, "Dearie, my sister, Miss Barrington, has had many disappointments, and she seems to have lost faith in the world, but I am sure that she means to be kind." Then the little lady added with a sigh, "I had so hoped you would want to stay with me, for I am very lonely now that Cherise is gone. She was nearly your age and this was her room, Shall I tell you about her?"

"Yes, lady."

Miss Dahlia clasped the brown hand lovingly as she began.

"Long ago I had a twin brother, whom I dearly loved, but he married a very beautiful girl, who sang at concerts, and my sister, Miss Barrington, who sometimes seems unjust, would not receive her into our home, and my brother, who was deeply hurt, never communicated with us again. Many years passed and then one day a little girl of ten came to our door with a letter. She said that her name was Cherise and that her father and mother were dead. It was my dear brother's child. My sister, Miss Barrington was in the city where she spends many of the autumn months, and so I kept the little thing and told no one about her. Those were indeed happy days for me. This room, which had dark furniture and draperies, I had decorated in blue and gold just for her, and how she loved it. With her golden curls and sweet blue eyes she looked like a fairy in her very own bower.

"Little Nan, you can't know what a joy Cherise was to me. We spent long hours together in the garden with our books, for I would allow no one else to teach her, but, when she was fourteen, her spirits slipped away and left me alone. I thought when you came that perhaps Cherise had led you here that I might have someone to love. I do wish you would stay, at least for a while."

Nan looked into the wistful, loving face and then she turned to gaze out of the window. She was silent for so long that Miss Dahlia was sure that she would say no, but when the gypsy girl spoke, she said: "I'll stay until the gold flowers fade out there in the garden."

"Thank you, dearie," and then impulsively the little lady added: "Try to love me, Nan, and I am sure that we will be happy together."

The days that followed were hard ones for the gypsy girl, who felt as a wild bird must when it is first imprisoned in a cage, and her heart was often rebellious.

"But I'll keep my word," she thought, "I'll stay till the gold flowers fade."

The elder Miss Barrington began at once to try to civilize Nan, and the result was not very satisfactory.

CHAPTER VII.

CIVILIZING GYPSY NAN.

The first day that Nan was strong enough to sit up Miss Barrington entered the room, followed by a maid, who was carrying a large box. The gypsy girl was seated by one of the windows, wrapped in a woolly blue robe that belonged to Miss Dahlia.

"Anne!" the cold voice was saying, "that is the name I have decided to call you. Nan is altogether too frivolous for a Christian girl, and that is what I expect you to become. In order that you may cease to look like a heathen as soon as possible, I have had your gypsy toggery stored in the attic and I have purchased for you dresses that are quiet and ladylike."

Then turning to the maid, she said: "Marie, you may open the box and spread the contents on the bed."

There were two dresses. One was a dark brown wool, made in the plainest fashion, and the other was a dull blue.

Nan's eyes flashed. "I won't wear those ugly things!" she cried. "You have no right to take my own beautiful dress from me." Miss Barrington drew her self up haughtily as she replied coldly,—

"You will wear the dresses that I provide, or you will remain in your room. It is my duty, I assure you, not my pleasure, to try to change your heathen ways."

So saying Miss Barrington departed.

As soon as they were alone Miss Dahlia went over to the side of Nan's chair, and smoothing the dark hair with a loving hand, she said, pleadingly: "Dearie, wear them just for a time. My sister will soon be going to the city and you shall have something pretty."

Then, since the girl's eyes were still rebellious, the little lady opened a drawer and taking out a box she gave it to Nan.

"Those ribbons and trinklets belonged to Cherise. She would be glad to have you wear them."

The box contained many hair ribbons, some of soft hues and others of warm, glowing colors. Too, there was a slender gold chain with a lovely locket of pearls forming a flower.

"Oh, how pretty, pretty!" the gypsy girl murmured, and then instinctively wanting to say thank you, and not knowing how, she kissed the wrinkled cheek of the dear old lady.

That was the beginning of happy times for these two. When Nan was able to be out in the garden, she had her first reading lesson, and how pleased she was when at last she could read a simple fairy tale quite by herself from the beginning to the end.

The elder Miss Barrington, who was interested in culture clubs, was luckily away much of the time, but one day something happened which made that proud lady deeply regret that she had tried to civilize a heathen gypsy.

It was Sunday and the two ladies were ready to start for church. Nan was to have accompanied them. A neat tailored suit had been provided for her Sunday wear, a pair of kid gloves and a blue sailor hat. That morning when the gypsy girl went up to her room, she found a maid there who informed her that she was to dress at once as the ladies would start for St. Martin's-by-the-sea in half an hour.

When she was alone, Nan put on the garment that was so strange to her and the queer stiff hat. She stood looking in the long mirror and her eyes flashed. She would not wear that ugly head dress. She was not a gorigo and she would not dress like one. She heard someone ascending the stairs, and, believing it to be Miss Barrington coming to command that she go to church with them, Nan darted out into the corridor and opening the first door that she came to, she entered a dark hall where she had never been before. A flight of wooden stairs was there and ever so quietly she stole up, and, opening another door at the top, she entered the attic. Then she stood still and listened. She heard faint voices far below. Evidently Miss Barrington was looking for her. Nan glanced about to see where she would hide if anyone came up the stairs but no one did, and soon she heard an automobile going down the drive.

Darting to a small window, to her relief, she saw that both ladies were on their way to church. Then suddenly she remembered something! She had given her word to dear Miss Dahlia that she would attend the morning service and she had never before broken a promise, but she could not, she would not wear that ugly suit and that stiff round hat. As she turned from the window, a flash of color caught her eye. There was an old trunk near and a bit of scarlet protruded from beneath the cover. With a cry of joy, Nan leaped to the spot and lifted the lid. Just as she had hoped, it was her own beautiful dress.

Gathering it lovingly in her arms, she started down the attic stairs, tiptoeing quietly lest she attract the attention of a maid.

Once in her room, she locked the door and joyously dressed in the old way, a yellow silk handkerchief wound about her flowing dark hair, and the gorgeous crimson and gold shawl draped about her shoulders.

No one saw the gypsy girl as she stole from the back door and into the garden-all-aglow. She picked a big, curly-yellow crysanthemum (for Miss Dahlia had told her to gather them whenever she wished) and she fastened it in the shawl. Then mounting her pony, she galloped down the highway. She was going to attend the morning services at the little stone church, St. Martin's-by-the-sea.

At the solemn moment when all heads were bowed in prayer, Nan reached the picturesque, ivy covered stone church and stood gazing wonderingly in at the open door.

Never before had this child of nature been in the portal of a church, and she felt strangely awed by the silence and wondered why the people knelt and were so still. Nan had never heard of prayer to an unseen God.

Her first impulse was to steal out again and gallop away up the mountain road where birds were singing, the sun glowing on red pepper berries, and everything was joyous. The gypsy girl could understand Nature's way of giving praise to its creator, but she had promised Miss Dahlia that she would attend the morning service, and so she would stay. Gazing over the bowed heads with joy she recognized one of them. Her beloved Miss

Dahlia and the dreaded Miss Ursula occupied the Barrington pew, which was near the chancel.

Tiptoeing down the aisle, she reached the pew just as the congregation rose to respond to a chanted prayer. Unfortunately Miss Ursula sat on the outside, and there was not room for Nan. She stood still and gazed about helplessly. A small boy in front of Miss Barrington had turned, and seeing Nan, he tugged on his mother's sleeve and whispered: "Look, Mummie, here's a real gypsy in our church." Miss Ursula turned also, and when she beheld Nan in that "heathen costume," her face became a deep scarlet, and the expression in her eyes was not one that should have been inspired by her recent devotions.

"Go home at once." she said, in a low voice, "and remain in your room until I return."

Nan left the church. She was glad, glad to be once more out in the sunshine. She did not want to know the God of the gorigo if He dwelt in that dreary, sunless place.

As she galloped down the coast highway, how she wished that she might ride up into the mountains and never return.

Then she thought of Miss Dahlia. Just for a fleeting moment she had caught that dear little lady's glance when Miss Barrington was dismissing her, and Nan was almost sure that Miss Dahlia's sweet grey eyes had twinkled.

"I will only have to stay until the gold blossoms fade," the girl thought a little later, as she wandered about the garden paths peering into the curly yellow crysanthemums, wondering how much longer they would last. With a sigh, Nan went indoors and up to her room.

Undressing, she placed the gown that she so loved in a bureau drawer, and then, to please Miss Dahlia she put on the simple blue cashmere and sat with folded hands waiting to hear in what manner she was to be punished.

CHAPTER VIII.

NAN'S PUNISHMENT.

Half an hour later Nan heard the automobile returning and she sighed resignedly. The gypsy girl's heart was rebellious, yet she would bear with it a little longer for Miss Dahlia's sake.

The door was opening, but Nan, with folded hands still gazed out of the window. A severe voice spoke:

"Anne, when I enter the room, I wish you to rise."

"Yes, lady," was the listless reply as the girl arose.

"And one thing more. I do not wish you to call me 'lady' in that gypsy fashion. If you wish to say Lady Ursula, you may do so. My English ancestry entitles me to that name."

Miss Barrington and Miss Dahlia then seated themselves, but Nan remained standing.

"Why don't you sit down?" the former asked impatiently.

"Sister," a gentle voice interceded, "Nan can't know our parlor manners, when she has been brought up in the big out-of-doors."

"She will soon have the opportunity to learn them, however," Miss Barrington said coldly, "for I have decided, since this morning's performance, to place Anne in a convent school. I find the task of Christianizing and civilizing a heathen more than I care to undertake."

"Oh, Sister Ursula, don't send Nan away," the other little lady implored. "Let me teach her. I will do so gladly."

"You!" The tone was scornful. "Do you suppose that you can succeed where I fail? No indeed, Anne shall tomorrow depart for a convent school which is connected with our church."

Then rising, she added: "We will now descend to the dining room and we will consider the subject closed."

Had the proud Miss Barrington glanced at the girl who was keeping so still, she might have seen a gleam in the dark eyes which showed that her spirit was not yet broken.

As they went down the wide stairway, Miss Dahlia slipped her hand over the brown one that hung listlessly at the girl's side. Nan understood that it was an assurance of the little lady's love, and her heart responded with sudden warmth.

All that afternoon Nan sat in a sheltered corner of the garden with a beautiful story that she was trying to read, but her thoughts were continually planning and plotting. She could not and would not be sent to a convent school. She was only staying to keep her promise to Miss Dahlia, but now that Miss Ursula was sending her away, she was freed from that promise.

Just then a maid appeared, saying: "Miss Barrington wishes to see you in the library at once. She's got a telegram from somewhere and she's all upset about it."

When Nan entered the stately library, she saw Miss Barrington standing near Miss Dahlia's chair, and the younger woman was saying: "But, Sister Ursula, it would be of no use for me to go. I know nothing of law and of things like that."

"I am quite aware of the fact," the older woman said, "and I had no intention whatever of requesting you to go, but it is most inconvenient for me to spend several months in the East just at this time. I am president of the Society for Civic Improvements, and an active and influential member in many other clubs, as you know." Then, noting that Nan had entered the room, she turned toward her as she said coldly: "Anne, I shall be obliged to leave for New York on the early morning train. A wealthy aunt has passed away, leaving a large fortune to my sister and myself, but unfortunately, the will is to be contested, which necessitates the presence of an heir who has some knowledge of legal matters. I may be away for several months, and so I will have to leave you in my sister's care, trusting that she will see the advisability of sending you to a convent school as soon as a suitable wardrobe can be prepared. That is all! You may now retire."

It had been hard for Nan to quietly listen to this glorious and astounding news. She did glance for one second at Miss Dahlia, and she was sure that she saw a happy light in those sweet grey eyes.

The next morning the household was astir at a very early hour, and at nine o'clock the automobile returned from the station and Miss Dahlia was in it alone.

Nan joyously ran across the lawn and caught the outstretched hands of the little lady.

"Oh, Miss Dahlia," the girl implored, "you aren't going to send me to a convent, are you? Because, if you do, I am going to run away."

"No, indeed, dearie," Miss Dahlia replied, as she sat on a marble bench near the fountain, and drew the girl down beside her.

Then she laughed as Nan had never heard her laugh before. There was real joy in it. "Dearie," she said, "I begged my sister to permit me to do what I could to try to civilize you while she is away, and, because her mind was so much occupied with other and weightier matters, she gave her consent, but she made me promise that you would attend service with me wearing proper clothes, and that I would teach you to sew and also lady-like manners."

"Oh, Miss Dahlia, I, will civilize fast enough for you, because I love you," the girl said, impulsively, as she pressed a wrinkled hand to her flush brown cheek.

"And I love you, Nan, you don't know how dearly, and you needn't civilize too much, if you don't want to. I love you just as you are. I am going to engage masters to come and teach you piano, singing and the harp or violin as you prefer."

The girl's dark eyes glowed happily as she exclaimed, "Oh, Miss Dahlia, how I love music; everything, every-where that sings; the brook, the bird, the wind in the trees! How glad I will be to learn to make music as they do."

Two wonderful weeks passed. A little French lady came to teach Nan languages, for which she had a remarkable aptitude, and when she began to sing as sweetly and naturally as the wood birds, Miss Dahlia was indeed delighted, and in the long evenings she taught the gypsy girl the songs that she used to sing. Too, there had been a shopping expedition to the village, and Nan had chosen a soft cashmere dress, the color of ripe cherries with the sun shining on them. At the beginning of the third week something happened which was destined to do much toward civilizing Nan.

CHAPTER IX.

THE LAD NEXT DOOR.

It was Saturday and lessons were over for the week. Of tutors and music masters there would be none all that glorious day. Miss Dahlia had awakened with a headache. Nan slipped into the darkened room and asked tenderly if there was something that she could do to help.

"No, dearie," the little lady replied, "I will just rest awhile. Go for a ride on Binnie if you wish. I will try to be down so that you need not have luncheon alone."

A few moments later the girl emerged from a vine-hung side entrance and stood looking about. She wore her cherry red dress and the yellow silk handkerchief, with its dangles, was about her head.

In her hand she held a book, "Ivanhoe." Miss Dahlia had been reading it aloud the night before, and the gypsy girl was eager to continue the story.

She would find a sheltered spot, she thought, and try to read it, although, as she well knew, many of the words were long and hard.

The Barrington estate contained several acres. Nan had never crossed to the high hedge that bounded it on the farther side from town.

Great old trees lured her and wondering what lay beyond the hedge, she started tramping in that direction singing a warbling song without words.

A great old pepper tree with its glowing red berries stood on the Barrington side, and Nan, gazing up, saw one wide branch curving in a way that would make of it a comfortable seat. Scrambling up, she was soon perched there. Then she peered through the thick foliage, trying to see what might be in the grounds beyond.

It was another picturesque home of Spanish architecture similar to the Barrington's with glowing gardens and artistic groupings of shrubbery and trees.

There was no sign of life about the place, and then Nan recalled having heard Miss Ursula say that it was the home of Mrs. Warren Widdemere a beautiful young widow possessing great wealth, who was traveling in

Europe trying to forget her recent bereavement. Mrs. Widdemere had a son who was in a military academy, and so, in all probability the place was unoccupied, the girl thought, as she opened her book, and began slowly and yet with increasing interest, to read.

Half an hour later she became conscious that there were voices near, and on the other side of the hedge. Glancing through the sheltering green, she beheld a woman in nurse's uniform who was pushing a wheeled chair, in which sat a boy of about 16. His face was pale and his expression listless; almost discouraged, Nan thought.

As they neared the tree, a bell rang from the house, and the nurse, leaving the chair, started up the garden path.

"Don't hurry back," the boy called languidly.

"This place will do for my sunbath as well as any other." Then he leaned back, and, closing his eyes, he sighed wearily.

Nan, prompted by pity and a desire to be friendly, broke a cluster of pepper berries and tossed them toward the chair. They fell lightly on the boy's folded hands. He opened his eyes and looked about, but he saw no one.

"Poor, poor boy!" Nan thought with a rush of tenderness. The gypsy girl always had the same pity when she saw anything that was wounded, and it was this tenderness in her nature that had compelled her to remain in the caravan for so long to protect the little cripple Tirol.

The sick lad, believing that a cluster of pepper berries had but fallen of its own accord once more leaned back and closed his eyes, but he opened them almost instantly and again looked about. From somewhere overhead he heard a sweet warbling bird-song. "Perhaps a mocking bird," he was thinking when the note changed to that of a meadowlark.

Gazing steadily at the tree ahead of him, he saw a gleam of red and then a laughing face peering between the branches.

"I see you! Whoever you are, come down!" His querulous voice held a command.

"Indeed sir. I don't have to," was the merry reply. "I am a bird with red and gold feathers and I shall remain in my tree."

The boy smiled. It was the first time that he had been interested in the five months since his father had died.

"I can see the glimmer of your plumage through the leaves," he called. Then changing his tone, he said pleadingly, "Lady Bird won't you please come down?"

Nan dropped lightly to the ground on the Widdemere side of the hedge.

The lad looked at the beautiful dark-skinned maiden, and then, little dreaming that he was speaking the truth, he said, "Why, Lady Bird, your dress makes you look like a gypsy."

"I am one!" the girl replied. "My name is Gypsy Nan. I am staying with the Barrington's for a time." Then her dark eyes twinkled merrily as she confided. "Miss Ursula Barrington is trying to civilize me, but she had to go away, and oh I am so glad! It isn't a bit nice to be civilized, is it?"

The boy laughed. "I know that I wouldn't be if I could help myself," he said. "I've always wished that I had been born a wild Indian or a pirate or something interesting."

Nan seated herself on a stump that would soon be covered with vines.

"I don't wonder you are sick," she said with renewed sympathy. "I would be smothered, I know, if I had to live all of the time in houses with so much velvet, and portieres shutting out the wind and the sun. Tell me what is your name?"

"I am Robert Widdemere," he replied, and then a shadow crept into the eyes that for a moment had been gleaming with amusement as he added:

"I'm never going to be well again. The doctor does not know what is the matter with me; no one does, but I can't eat, and so I might as well hurry up and die."

The girl looked steadily at the lad for a moment and then she said, "Robert Widdermere, you ought to have more courage than that. Of course you'll die if you're just going to weakly give up. I don't believe that you're sick at all. I think you have been too much civilized. Now I'll tell you what you do. Eat all you can, and get strong fast, and then we will ride horseback over the mountains and I'll run you a race on the coast highway."

"That would be great!" the boy exclaimed and again his eyes glowed with a new eagerness.

The girl sprang up. "Hark!" she said, "the old mission bells are telling that it is noon. I must go or Miss Dahlia will be waiting lunch.

"Good-bye, Robert Widdemere, I'll come again."

The lad watched the gleam of red disappearing through a gate in the hedge which he had pointed out. Then a new determination awakened in his heart. Perhaps it was cowardly to give up and die, just because he was so lonesome, so lonesome for the dad who had been the dearest pal a boy could ever have.

Robert's father had died five months before and his mother, a rather frivolous young widow, who had always cared more for society than for her home, had placed her sixteen-year-old son in a military academy and had departed for Paris to try to forget her loss in the gay life of that city, but Robert had been unable to forget, and day after day he had grieved for that father who had been his pal ever since he could first remember. These two had been often alone as the wife and mother had spent much time at week-end house-parties in the country places of her wealthy friends. No wonder was it that the boy felt that he had lost his all.

At last, worn with the grief which he kept hidden in his heart, his health had broken and a cablegram from his mother had bidden him go with a nurse to their California home at San Seritos, adding, that if he did not recover in one month, she would return to the States, but since it was only the beginning of the gay season in Paris, she did hope that he would endeavor to get well as soon as possible.

The lad had read the message with a lack of interest and to the attending physician he had said: "Kindly cable my mother to remain in France as I am much better, but that I shall stay in California for the winter."

The kindly doctor wondered at the message. He had but recently come to San Seritos and he did not understand the cause, as the old physician whose place he had taken, would have understood it.

Robert Widdemere, without the loving tenderness of a mother to help him bear his great loneliness, did not care to live until he met Gypsy Nan. When she had looked at him so reprovingly with those dark eyes that could be so serious or dancingly merry, and had said that it was cowardly for him to give up so weakly he had decided that she was right. He ought to want to live to carry out some of the splendid things that his father had begun if for nothing else, but now there was something else! He wanted to get strong soon that he might ride horseback with Nan over the mountains.

When Miss Squeers returned to push the wheeled chair and its usually listless occupant back to the house she was surprised to note that he looked up with a welcoming smile. "Nurse," he said, "do you know, I am actually hungry. Don't give me broth tonight. I want some regular things to eat, beefsteak and mashed potatoes."

A query over the wire brought a speedy reply from the physician: "Give the lad whatever he asks for and note the result."

The next day Doctor Wainridge called and the lad asked: "Doctor, is there any real reason why I cannot walk?"

"None whatever, son, that I know of," the gentleman replied, "except that you have been too weak to stand, but if you continue with the menu that you ordered last night, you will soon be able to enter the Marathon races. There is nothing physically wrong with you, lad. I decided that you had made up your mind that you did not care to get well."

The boy looked around and finding that they were alone, he confided, "I did feel that way, doctor, but now I wish to get well soon, and be a pirate or a gypsy or something uncivilized."

"Great!" the doctor said, as he arose to go.

On his way home he wondered what had aroused Robert's interest in life, but neither he nor the nurse could guess.

CHAPTER X.

"LADY RED BIRD."

Again it was Saturday. Every day during the past week Robert had walked, only a few steps at first, but each day going a little farther. Too, each afternoon he had eagerly watched at the pepper tree for the appearance of his Lady Red Bird, but she had not come.

"Perhaps she only comes on Saturday," he thought as he sat alone in his wheeled chair waiting and watching.

Suddenly a rose hurled over the hedge and fell on his book.

"Oho, Lady Red Bird," he called joyously. "I can't see you, but I know that you are there. Please come over on this side."

The gate opened ever so little and Nan peered through.

Then skipping in front of him, she cried, with her dark eyes aglow, "Why, Robert Widdemere, you don't look like the same boy. What have you done? You look almost well."

"I am," the lad replied, smiling radiantly. "I am going to be well enough to ride up the mountain road with you on Thanksgiving morning, and then I will surely have something to be thankful for."

Gypsy Nan clapped her hands. "And we'll ride a race on the hard sand close to the sea."

"Great!" ejaculated the lad. "That will be two weeks from to-day. I'll have to order my portion of beefsteak and mashed potatoes doubled, I guess." Then he added with a merry twinkle, "Promise me that you'll wear the gypsy-looking dress."

"Oh, I will," Nan cried, "for I love it." Then she added, "Robert Widdemere, you don't believe that I am truly a gypsy, do you?"

The lad shook his head and his brown eyes were laughing. "Why, of course not Lady Red Bird! Gypsies are interesting enough, in their way, but they are not like you. They are thieves — "

The girl sprang up from the stump on which she had been seated, and her eyes flashed. "They are not all thieves, Robert Widdemere," she cried, "and many of them are just as good and kind as gorigo could be. Manna Lou was a beautiful young gypsy woman long ago, when I first remember her, and she could have had a much happier life if she had hot chosen of her own free will to care for that poor little cripple boy Tirol, and for the motherless Nan. I wish I had not run away from the caravan now. I hate the gorigo, who always call my people thieves!" Then turning to the amazed and speechless lad, she inquired with flashing eyes, "Are there no thieves among your people? Indeed there are, but they are not all called thieves! My Manna Lou taught me not to steal, and I have never taken even a flower that did not belong to me. I'm going back, Robert Widdemere! I'm going back to Manna Lou."

The girl burst into a passion of tears as she turned toward the gate. The lad, deeply touched, forgetting his weakness, was at her side and placing a hand on her arm, he implored, "Oh Lady Red Bird, forgive me. I see now how wrong it is to condemn a whole race because of the few. Promise me that you won't go back. It is knowing you that has helped me to get well, and if you go away, I will be lonelier than ever."

The boy had returned to his chair and he looked suddenly pale and tired. Nan's heart was touched, and she said, "Robert Widdemere, now that you know I am really a gypsy, do you still care for my friendship?"

"I care more to be your friend, than for anything else in the whole world," the lad said sincerely.

"Then I'll not go back to the caravan," she promised, a smile flashing through the tears. "Goodbye, Robert Widdemere. I'll come again tomorrow."

These two little dreamed that the nurse, Miss Squeers, hidden behind a clump of shrubbery, had seen and heard all that had passed, nor could they know that upon returning to the house, she had at once written to the lad's mother.

When on the day following, Nan returned to the little gate in the hedge, Robert Widdemere was not seen. The nurse, having overheard the planned meeting had ordered the horses hitched to the easiest carriage and had insisted that the lad accompany her on a drive. He was restless when he realized that they were not to return at the hour he had expected his Lady Red Bird to visit him, and indeed, when at last, they did turn into the long winding drive leading to his handsome home, he was so worn and weary from having fretted because he had been forced to do something he did not wish to do, that he had a fever and had to go at once to bed. Miss Squeers sent for the doctor and drawing him aside, she confided all she had found out. If she had expected an ally, she was greatly disappointed.

"That's great!" Doctor Wainridge exclaimed, his kindly face shining. "Nothing could be better. A tonic is powerless compared to a lad's interest in a lassie. But if he was so much better only yesterday, because of this friendship, what has caused the set-back?"

Miss Squeer's thin lips were pressed together in a hard line. "Doctor Wainridge, you evidently do not realize that this young person is a real gypsy. You wouldn't have doubted it if you could have seen her black eyes flash yesterday when Robert Widdemere spoke disparagingly of the race."

The physician looked interested, and somewhat amused. "Indeed, I could imagine it!" he said with assurance. "I had a gypsy boy for a patient once and a fiery tempered lad, he was, but I liked him. The fact is, I admire much about their life, not everything of course. They do a little too much horse trading, and sometimes they even trade without the owners being aware of it." At that he laughed, appearing not to notice that a ramrod could not be standing stiffer or more erect than was Miss Squeers. He continued as though amused at the memory. "It was down south when I was practicing there. One of the southern colonels had a thoroughbred horse. He boasted about it on all occasions, but when the gypsies came and passed they had traded an old boney nag with the colonel. He found it in the paddock where his prize racer had been locked in securely the night before."

"Well," Miss Squeers snapped, "I hope you are not upholding such conduct."

The good-natured physician shook his head, but his eyes were still twinkling. "No, indeed not!" he said emphatically. "That manner of horse trading is not to be condoned in the slightest degree."

"Trading?" With biting sarcasm Miss Squeers spoke the word. "Stealing, you mean. That's what they all are, thieves and liars." Then with a self-righteous expression on her drawn, white face, the woman continued: "Mrs. Widdemere puts her entire trust in my judgment and until she comes to relieve me, I shall not permit her son to again speak to that gypsy girl."

The doctor narrowed his eyes, gazing thoughtfully at the speaker. When she paused he exclaimed "Good Lord, Miss Squeers, what possible harm could a girl of thirteen or fourteen do a sixteen year old boy? I have heard the story of the protege of the Misses Barrington. Indeed it has been rumored about that she is very beautiful and rarely talented. My wife is well acquainted with the woman who is instructing the girl on the harp and she has only enthusiastic praise for the gifts with which she has been endowed. Nature is the mother of us all, and is no respector of persons."

"Then you advise me to permit this friendship to continue even though I know it would greatly displease Mrs. Widdemere who is among the proudest of proud women?"

The doctor thoughtfully twirled the heavy charm on his watch chain. "If we have to choose between losing our patient and displeasing a vain mother, I prefer the latter. You can see for yourself that the boy has had a set-back. This is most discouraging to me. And, as his physician, I shall have to ask, as long as I have the case, and the boy's mother cabled me to take it, that he be given his freedom in the matter. Do not again force him to go for a drive with you unless it is his wish to do so. I will call again tomorrow."

The nurse watched him go with a steely expression in her sharp green-blue eyes. Next she walked to a calender and marked on it the probable day when she might expect a response to the letter she had written Mrs. Widdemere.

Then she went upstairs and found her patient tossing restlessly. After all, she decided it might be better for her to follow the doctor's orders. She would not have long to wait for orders from one higher in authority.

CHAPTER XI.

THE DOCTOR TAKES A HAND.

Doctor Wainridge had done a little thinking on his own part and he arrived at the Widdemere home early the next morning. Finding that the boy was in a listless state, from which he had been aroused only by his interest in his new friend, the physician, after dismissing the nurse, sat down by the bed-side and took the thin hand in his own.

"Robert, lad," he began in a low voice that could not possibly be overheard by an intentional or unintentional eavesdropper, "I hear that you have made the acquaintance of that little gypsy lady who is staying next door." The boy looked up with almost startled inquiry. He had not supposed that their meeting had been observed. Then a hard expression shadowed his eyes. "Huh, I might have known that sly cat would pry around. I suppose she told you."

The good-natured doctor wanted to laugh aloud. He quite agreed with the boy's description of the nurse, but, of course, it would not be ethical to permit the patient to know this and so he said, assuming an expression of professional interest merely: "Miss Squeers mentioned it to me, Robert, and of course, in her capacity as nurse, she feels, in the absence of your mother, that she should try, if possible, to influence you against a friendship that your mother might not wish you to make."

The boy's eyes flashed and he drew himself to a sitting posture. "Doctor Wainridge," he said vehemently, "how can I ever get well if I am kept a prisoner with a jailor whom I hate, hate, hate! Can't you dismiss Miss Squeers from my case and just look after me yourself. Gee whiz, Doctor Wainridge, aren't there servants enough around this place to make me some broth and give me a bath."

The doctor glanced at the closed door and put his fingers on his lips as a suggestion that the boy speak in a lower voice. "I cannot dismiss Miss Squeers," he said, "because in your mother's cable to me she asked that she be called, but, of course, as you know, a doctor's orders must be carried out, and so I now order, that, until your mother dismisses me, you are to see as much of the little gypsy girl as possible, if you find her companionship amusing. You are merely children and as such need young companionship." Then, after feeling the lad's pulse and taking his temperature, he said loud and cheerily, "Well, Robert Widdemere, you feel pretty well I judge. Fever's all gone and you look rested."

"There wasn't anything the matter with me yesterday only I was mad, mad clear through." The boy cast a vindictive glance at the closed door on the other side of which they could both visualize a wrathful nurse, trying, if possible, to hear the conference she had been barred from. Then the boy confessed. "It was this way, Doctor Wainridge, that nice girl, Lady Red Bird, the one next door, told me that she would come back to the hedge yesterday afternoon to ask how I was getting on, and that nurse must have heard, for she took me driving and kept me away until I was so angry that it wore me all out, and I had a fever. Now, what worries me is, will Lady Red Bird ever come back again? It isn't a bit likely that she will. Girls have too much pride to chase after a fellow, if he isn't there when he says he will be. She'll think I'm a cad. I just know she won't come again, and I wouldn't blame her if she didn't."

"Neither would I blame her, Robert," the doctor agreed. "Now, laddie, listen to me. If you will rest all this morning and eat a good lunch and not be wrathful at your nurse whatever she may say or do, I'll come over this afternoon and take you to call on your new friend. I've been planning for ever so long to drop in and see Miss Dahlia. I've been their family physician more years than I like to remember. Well, sonny, how does, that plan strike you."

The boy looked up brightly. "Bully," he ejaculated. Then anxiously he inquired, "Shall you tell the nurse?"

"I'll tell her to get you ready for a drive as I shall call for you at two. Then I will let Miss Dahlia know that I am to call on her at two-thirty and would like to meet her protêge."

The old doctor was indeed pleased to see how quickly his suggestion brightened the lad's face.

45

Reaching out a thin hand, he took the big brown one as he said; "Doc, you're a trump! I needn't feel that I haven't a friend when you're at the wheel. Now I'm going to rest hard until noon."

CHAPTER XII.

A PLEASANT CALL.

Miss Squeers found it hard to follow orders that were so against her own judgment. She well knew Mrs. Widdemere, for had she not been in that home during the illness of Robert's father and had she not found his mother a woman after her own heart! "If a person is born an aristocrat," the nurse told herself, "she ought to act like one and be haughty and proud. How would a peacock look trying to put herself on a social footing with a pullet?"

All the time that she was assisting Robert Widdemere to dress for the drive that he was to take with Doctor Wainridge, the woman's thin colorless lips grew tighter and thinner. The physician had not told where he was going to take their patient, but she knew, as well as if she had been able to hear through the closed door. She consoled herself with the knowledge that her turn to triumph would come in time. They did not know, however much they might suspect it, that she had written the mother all that she knew of this disgraceful friendship. Doctor Wainridge would be peremptorially dismissed, of that Miss Squeers was certain. For that matter the doctor was sure of the same thing, but what he hoped was that his patient should by that time be so far along on the road to recovery that he would not be harmed by his mother's anger or subsequent action. That Mrs. Widdemere would forbid the friendship, he well knew. But his office, at present, was to help the lad to rouse himself from the indifferent stupor into which he had fallen since his father's death.

The doctor arrived at two, and for half an hour they drove about the picturesque country lane on either side of which were the vast estates of the wealthy dwellers of the far famed foot-hill section.

At length they left the highway and turned into the drive leading to the Barrington home. The physician was saying: — "I was up in the big city when it all happened and so another doctor was called when the accident occured. I am referring to the accident which brought the gypsy girl into the home where I presume she is to remain." Then he laughed. "It is well for the girl that the haughty older sister has gone away for an indefinite stay for she had undertaken, so the story goes, to civilize and Christianize this little heathen."

The boy nodded. "Lady Red Bird told me. She said she was just ready to run away because they were going to put her in a convent school, when a telegram came and Miss Ursula Barrington left at once for the East."

As they neared the house, they saw a very pretty sight. The girl of whom they had been talking, looking more then ever like a gypsy in the costume she had worn when she had first arrived, was dancing up and down the paths of the glowing garden shaking her tambourine, as she had danced on that never-to-be-forgotten day when she had been there with little Tirol. Nearby on a bench the younger Miss Barrington sat with her lace crochet now and then dropping it to her lap to smile at the girl. Suddenly she called. "Nan, dearie, the company has come." The girl dropped to a marble bench, but a side glance toward the drive showed her that both the doctor and the boy had witnessed her performance.

"I don't care, Miss Dahlia," she said, tossing her dark hair back and out of her eyes, "I put this dress on purposely that Robert Widdemere might see I'm not ashamed that I am a gypsy. I'm proud, proud, proud because I belong to Manna Lou."

"Of course you are, dearie," the gentle little woman rose and advanced to greet the newcomers.

"Doctor Wainridge," she said, "I'm so glad that you have come to meet our dear adopted daughter. It was a real regret to me that you were out of town at the time of the accident, if something which results in great joy and happiness can be called by so formidable a name. And this," she held out a slender white hand toward the glowing girl, "is our Nan."

The doctor, whose broad-brimmed black felt was under one arm, shook hands with Miss Dahlia and then with the girl. Turning, he beamed on the lad as he said, "Surely, Miss Barrington, you remember this boy, although you may not have seen him recently."

"Indeed I do! Robert, how you have grown." Then noting his pale face, she said with kindly solicitude, "You are not yet strong. Shall we go into the house? Would it not be more comfortable there?"

But the doctor, after glancing at his watch replied: "I fear that I cannot remain today, as I have other patients to see, but if you are willing to entertain your young neighbor, I will return for him in just one hour."

Robert's face brightened. "That's great of you, doctor, to leave me in so pleasant a place." Then turning to Miss Dahlia who was looking at him pityingly, he confessed. "I'm bored to death at home with that specter of a nurse watching over me for all the world like a vulture swinging around the head of some poor creature that it expects is soon to die."

The doctor had been glancing about. There was a summer house near in which there were comfortably cushioned rustic chairs and a table. It was where Miss Dahlia and Nan had their daily lessons.

"That would be a pleasant place for you children to go for a real visit, isn't it?" he suggested. Miss Dahlia nodded smilingly and Nan led the way to the summer house. Miss Dahlia then walked at the doctor's side toward his car as she wished to ask his advice about her headaches.

"Isn't he a great sport?" Robert looked after his friend and ally admiringly, then he blurted out: — "Lady Red Bird, that sly cat of a nurse was trying to keep us apart. That's why I wasn't at the gate in the hedge yesterday. If I'd been strong enough I would have walked over here when I reached home and explained, but I was lots worse."

The lad glanced anxiously into the flushed face of the girl. He feared she was hurt with him. "I say, Miss Nan, you'll forgive my not being there. I wouldn't be such a cad, if I could help it. You know that, don't you?"

He was greatly relieved with the reply which was, "I wasn't there myself, Robert Widdemere. Miss Dahlia had one of her headaches and was so sick I didn't wan't to leave her. I was sure you would understand." Then, quickly changing the subject, she added. "This is a real comfortable chair. It's where Miss Dahlia sits when she teaches me to read. Oh, I love reading," she exclaimed, "and stories. I used to make them up out of my head to tell Little Tirol and the other children. Little wild foxes I called them."

There was a sudden far away wistful expression in the girl's dark eyes as she gazed out of the vine-hung door of the summer house, and the lad watching her, wondered that he had ever doubted that she was truly a gypsy. Surely, in that costume, there could be no question about it.

He said gently, "Lady Red Bird, I believe you sometimes wish you could go back to the old life." She turned wide startled eyes toward him as she replied in a tense voice, "I'm going back when the black dragon comes again. I won't stay here with her. I won't be civilized for her. She doesn't love me like Miss Dahlia does."

"But doesn't the wild gypsy life lure you?" the boy leaned forward interested. "I always imagine it as romantic and carefree."

Again the girl looked at him startled, then replied in a low voice. "Would you think it was romantic to have to do everything that a cruel, black-hearted Anselo Spico and his demon mother said to do? Would you call it being carefree when you were thrashed till the blood came if you wouldn't dance at the gorigo inns?

"I staid till little Tirol died. Anselo Spico had to beat me first, before he could get at that poor little cripple. I staid to take little Tirol's beatings, but when he was dead, I ran away and came here."

Robert Widdemere hardly knew what to say. "Lady Red Bird, I thought you told me you were proud of being a gypsy and that you loved the life."

There was an instant change and springing up she flung her arms wide with almost a wistful cry—"I love living out in the open, with only the starry sky for a roof, and the branches of trees swaying, swaying over my head when I sleep. I love to ride on my pony Binnie away, away, away, to feel my hair blowing in the wind and to have nothing to do but live."

Robert sighed. "I'd like right well to be that kind of a gypsy," he said. "I'd like to wander away, away, away from nurses and houses and routine studies."

Miss Dahlia appeared in the door and she was followed by a maid with a tray. "I thought you children might like a tea party," she said, "and if you do not mind, I will join you."

The hour was soon up and the doctor bore away a very thoughtful lad. "Lady Red Bird is a real gypsy," he was thinking, "and I don't believe she will civilize."

CHAPTER XIII.

MYSTERIOUS REVELATIONS.

That was the beginning of a series of visits. Sometimes these two planned to meet on the beach and always Nan wore her gypsy dress. Somehow she was determined that her new friend should not forget who she really was.

A week had passed and they were becoming well acquainted. Being constantly questioned about her past life, Nan had told many stories of the gypsies and adventures.

They were sitting in the sun on the sand one morning and Nan was being especially thoughtful.

"A penny for your thoughts, Lady Red Bird?" the boy asked.

"I was wondering where I will find the caravan when I run away." She looked up, a strange eagerness in her expressive dark eyes. "I must find them when I am eighteen for Manna Lou is to tell me then about my own mother."

Hesitatingly the boy suggested: "Would you be greatly disappointed if she were to tell you that you are not a real gypsy?" He almost feared that she would flare at him wrathfully as she had that first time, when he had scoffed at the idea of her being one. But instead, she turned toward him dark eyes in which there was the light of a simple conviction. "There is no question about that. I asked Manna Lou, and she said—'It is real gypsy blood that has given you that dark skin Leichen Nan.' But more, she would not tell. Manna Lou neverlied."

The boy leaned forward eagerly. "But she promised to tell you more when you were eighteen?"

"Yes."

"Then there is something to tell."

"Yes. But I am a gypsy."

The boy smiled. "I believe you would be disappointed if you found that you were not."

"But I am! Manna Lou said so. Manna Lou does not lie." It was always like arguing in a circle. From whatever point they started, they swung back to that same statement which was final in the mind of the girl. Suddenly the boy asked; "Have you always lived in California?"

"Oh no, no!" Nan replied. "We fled from Rumania. That is my country. There are many gypsies in that land across the sea. Manna Lou said there are more than 200,000 gypsies."

One word had attracted and held the attention of the lad. "Lady Red Bird, why did you say 'fled?' Did your band have to leave Rumania?"

She gleamed at him quickly, suspiciously. Then she replied dully, "I don't know. I suppose so! Anselo Spico and his queen mother Mizella, they do wrong things. They steal—" she paused, and the boy put in suggestively: "Do they steal white children?"

Scornfully the girl flung back. "No, never! Horses here in this country, but over there it was more—I never knew, something that made Anselo Spico afraid. We traveled day and night."

The boy said nothing but sat poking at the sand with a stick. It looked very mysterious to him. "You don't know what that Spico, or whatever it is you call him; you don't know what crime he had committed that he left your native country so suddenly?"

The girl shook her head. "And we didn't stop in the East where we landed, but we came right on and on and on till we reached California."

The boy was thinking aloud. "It seems strange to me that the authorities where the boats stop would permit wandering bands of gypsies to land in this country without knowing what they come for, or why they are leaving their own native land."

"What do you mean, authorities? What are they?" The girl was plainly perplexed.

"Why when a big vessel arrives at Castle Garden in New York, every passenger has been given a permit to land from Ellis Island where they first stop. Oh, there's a lot of red tape before anyone can come ashore, and I should think a whole band of gypsies would have considerable difficulty passing the examiners, that is what I mean by authorities."

Still the girl looked at him blankly as one who did not understand. "We landed in the night on a lonely marshy shore. Florida they called it. The sailing barge that brought us across the sea left before daybreak, and when the sun came up we were in our caravans riding across a flat lonely country. We saw very few people because we slept days and passed through the villages at night. The gorigo police sometimes followed us to see that we kept going until we were out of the town but nobody stopped us. Then, for weeks and weeks we were crossing the wide sandy desert. We camped a long time in the Rocky Mountains. I never did understand that, I mean why we seemed to be hiding. I thought maybe Anselo Spico had stolen something and we were waiting until it would be safe to go on, but I heard Vestor report one night, when he came back from town that there had been no mail from Rumania and so I supposed that we had been waiting there long enough for Anselo Spico to write someone in Rumania and that we were waiting for the reply. At last it came and the message in that letter angered him terribly. He seized a whip and began to lash poor little Tirol. I threw myself on the child and he began to beat me. It was his Queen Mother Mizella, who stopped him by saying. I never forgot the words though they meant nothing to me. 'Bedone with that! You're like to kill her as may line your purse yet.' He snarled an answer, but he let us both alone after that or at least he never beat me again."

Robert Widdemere was more than ever convinced that Nan had been stolen as a child and that the gypsies were hoping someday to receive a rich reward for her, but what he could not understand was why, if that were true, it had been so long in coming.

If she had own relations in Rumania, they surely would have been glad to pay the ransom money as soon as they found the whereabouts of the child.

But of his thoughts, he said nothing. After a few moments, he asked; "What did you do next, Lady Red Bird?"

"Our caravan left the mountains and we traveled slowly westward. Manna Lou was kinder to me than ever before, and she taught me to play on a banjo which she said had belonged to my father. She did not know much about it, but I was so glad, glad to have it."

The girl's face darkened. "That was the last mean thing Anselo Spico did to me. He found me playing the banjo, and it seemed to anger him, or some memory was called up by it that he did. Anyhow he seized it and smashed it to pieces on a rock. How I've hated him ever since!"

Again there was one of the swift changes, and Nan turned toward the boy a face softened and beautified with tender memories. "My father played before the Queen of Rumania once and received a medal. Manna Lou told me."

The boy was indeed puzzled. "It's all a mystery and I'm afraid I won't be able to fathom it," he told himself.

"And now I am to be a musician, and I shall play before a queen," the girl leaped to her feet and was dancing about on the hard sand, startling to flight a flock of shining winged white-gulls that circled in the air over the sea. The boy also rose and feeling much stronger, he tried to dance, but was soon out of breath and laughingly sank back on the sand higher up where it was dry and warm.

"What I need," he said to himself, "is a costume to match Lady Red Bird's. Then I will be able to dance with her."

The idea pleased him, and he thought of it, smiling to himself.

At last the hour came for their parting. "Remember our agreement. Tomorrow will be Thanksgiving and we are to go for a horseback ride." Then catching both hands of the girl, the boy looked into her laughing eyes as he said with sincere earnestness. "If I have indeed regained my strength, I have no one to thank but Lady Red Bird."

"Oh, yes you have. It was Doctor Wainridge who brought you here. You must thank him as well."

"And also dear gentle Miss Dahlia," the lad concluded, "Good-bye until tomorrow."

CHAPTER XIV.

THE MOUNTAIN RIDE.

Thanksgiving came and at the appointed hour Nan was waiting at the beach gate when she saw a gypsy riding toward her. Nan's first thought was one of terror, for the approaching horseman looked as Anselo Spico had when arrayed in his best, a blue velvet corduroy suit, a scarlet silk sash and a wide felt hat edged with bright dangles.

"Oh, Robert Widdemere!" Nan cried, when she saw who it really was. "You looked so like Anselo Spico as you rode along by the sea, that I was about to run and hide. Where did you get that costume?"

"At a shop in town where one may procure whatever one wishes for a masquerade," the laughing lad replied as he leaped to the ground and made a deep, swinging bow with his gay hat.

"I like it, Lady Red Bird," he enthusiastically declared, "and I do believe that I will purchase this outfit. Won't we create a stir in the countryside as we ride together down the Coast Highway."

Nan laughed joyously. "It becomes you, Robert Widdemere," she said. It was hard for the girl to believe that the handsome, flushed youth at her side was the same pale sickly lad whom she had first met less than a month before.

During that time these two had become well acquainted, taking short walks together and reading Ivanhoe while they rested. Miss Dahlia found that her pupil was making remarkable progress under her new tutor, moreover she liked the youth with his frank, good-looking face and she was glad to have Nan companied by someone near her own age.

Miss Dahlia appeared at the beach gate to see them off on their long planned ride and she called after them, "Robert, lad, be sure to come back and share our Thanksgiving dinner."

"Thank you, Miss Dahlia, I would like to," the youth replied doffing his hat. Then the little lady watched them ride away and turn up the mountain road.

In her heart there was a strange misgiving that she could not understand. "What if her sister, Miss Ursula, should suddenly return," she thought. Then indeed would Miss Dahlia be censored for having permitted Nan to again assume the raiment of a heathen.

Never before had Nan seemed more charming to the lad than she did on that glorious morning when side by side they rode up a narrow canon road leading toward the mountains.

"See, Nan," the young philosopher called, "life is full of contrasts. Now we are in a blaze of warmth and sunlight, and, not a stone's throw ahead of us, is the darkness and dampness of the canon, where the pine trees stand so solemn and still, like sentinels guarding the mysteries that lie beyond."

The girl drew rein and gazed with big dark eyes at the boy. During the past month she had learned his many moods. In a serious voice she said. "I sometimes wonder how we dare go on, since we do not know the trail that is just ahead. I don't mean here," she lifted one hand from her horse's head and pointed toward the high walled canon in front of them. "I mean, I wonder how we dare go along life's trail when it is, so often, as though we are blind-folded."

The boy's face brightened. "Nan," he said, with a note of tenderness in his voice which the girl always noticed when he spoke of his father. "Did I ever tell you how my father loved the writings of Henry Van Dyke? It didn't matter what they were about, fishing, or hiking, or philosophising. My father felt that they were kin, because they both so loved the great out-of-doors. Just now, when you wondered how we dare go ahead when we cannot know what awaits us on life's trail, I happened to recall a few lines which Dad so often used to recite. They are from Van Dyke's poem called 'God of the Open Air.'"

The boy gazed at the girl as though he were sure of her appreciation of all he was saying. "It is a long poem and a beautiful one. I'll read it to you someday, but the part I have in mind tells just that how everything in nature has, planted deep in its being, a trust that the Power that created it will also care for it and guide it well. This is it:

"By the faith that the wild flowers show when they bloom unbidden;

By the calm of the river's flow to a goal that is hidden.

By the strength of the tree that clings to its deep foundation,

By the courage of bird's light wings on the long migration

(Wonderful spirit of trust that abides in Nature's breast.)

Teach me how to confide, and live my life, and rest."

"It is very beautiful," Nan said in a low voice and then, starting their horses, they entered the shadow of the mountain walls and slowly began the ascent.

The trail became so narrow that they had to ride single file for a long time. Each was quietly thinking, but at last they reached a wide place where the mountain brook formed a pool and at the girl's suggestion they dismounted to get a drink of the clear cold water.

"How peaceful and still it is here," Nan said as she sat on a moss covered rock, and, folding her hands, listened to the murmuring sounds of trickling water, rustling leaves, and soughing of the soft breeze in the pines.

Robert, standing with his arms folded, had been gazing far down the trail which they had just climbed, but chancing to glance at the girl he saw a troubled expression in her dark beautiful face. Sitting on a rock near her, the boy leaned forward as he asked eagerly. "Nan, you aren't longing for the old life, are you?"

She turned toward him with a smile that put his fears at rest. "Not that, Robert Widdemere. I was wondering if I dare ask you a question?"

"Why Lady Red Bird, of course you may. I will answer it gladly."

The boy little dreamed how hard a question it was to be. For another moment the girl was silent, watching the water that barely moved in the pool at her feet. Then in a very low voice she said; — "We gypsies do not believe in a God."

Although unprepared for this statement, the lad replied by asking, "What then do your people believe gave life to all this?" He waved an arm about to include all nature.

"They believe that there are unseen spirits in streams and woods that can harm them, if they will. Sometimes, when a storm destroyed our camp, we tried to appease the wrath of the spirit of the tempest with rites and charms. That was all. Manna Lou had heard of the gorigo God, and often she told little Tirol and me about that one great Power, but if we asked questions, she would sadly reply 'Who can know?'"

"Manna Lou was right in one way, Lady Red Bird, we cannot know, perhaps, but deep in the soul of each one of us has been implanted a faith and trust just as the poem tells. I do know that some Power, which I call God, brought me here and so sure I can trust that same Power to care for me and guide me if I have faith and trust."

There was a sudden brightening of the girl's face, "Oh, Robert Widdemere," she said, "I am so glad I asked you. I understand now better how it is, I, also, shall trust and have faith."

She arose and mounted on her pony and they began climbing the steeper trail which led to the summit of the low mountain.

At last they rode out into the sunlight, and, dismounting, stood on the peak of the trail.

Such beauty of scene as there was everywhere about them. Beyond the coast range, across a wide valley, there was still a higher and a more rugged mountain range and beyond that, in the far distance, a third, the peaks of which were scarcely visible in the haze and clouds.

Then they turned toward the sea, which, from that high point could be seen far beyond the horizon that they had every day on the beach. "Lady Red Bird," the boy laughed, "you will think me very dull today, I fear, but I can't help philosophising a bit at times. I was just thinking that when troubles crowd around us, it would be a wonderful thing, if, in our thoughts, we could climb to a high place and look down at them, we would find that, after all, they were not very large nor very important."

"Things do look small, surely," the girl said. "See the town nestling down there. The church steeple seems very little from here."

"I see the pepper tree where we first met," the lad turned and took the girl's hand. "I shall always think of you as my Lady Red Bird," he told her. Hand in hand they continued to stand as brother and sister might.

"And I see our marble fountain glistening in the sun," Nan declared. Suddenly the boy's clasp in the girl's hand tightened. "Look, quick," he said pointing downward, "there is a limousine turning from the highroad up into our drive. Who do you suppose is coming to call?"

"Perhaps it is your doctor," Nan suggested.

The lad laughed. "No indeed. For one thing he rides in an open run-about, and for another, he told me that since I had made up my mind to get well, he would have nothing more to do with me. There are enough truly sick people he said, who need his attention."

"Then, who can it be?" Nan persisted, but the lad merrily declared that he knew not and cared not. After gazing for a moment at the girl who was still looking down at the highway he exclaimed with mingled earnestness and enthusiasm. "Nan, you don't know how much it means to me, to have a sister like you, a friend, or a pal, the name doesn't matter. You're going to fill the place, in a way, that Dad held, and truly he was the finest man that ever trod the earth. Often he said to me 'Son, when you give your word, stand by it. I would rather have my boy honest and dependable, than have him president,' and I'm going to try, Nan, to become just such a man as was my father."

The girl's gaze had left the road and she looked straight into the clear blue-grey eyes of the boy at her side. "I am glad, Robert Widdemere," she said, "for I could never be proud of a friend whose word could not be depended upon."

The boy caught both of the girl's hands in his as he said, "Nan, listen to me, you have no older brothers to take care of you, and as long as I shall live, I want you to think of me as one to whom you can always come. It doesn't matter who tries to separate us, Nan, no one ever shall, I give you my word."

Tears sprang to the eyes of the girl, but that she need not show the depth of her emotion, she called laughingly, "Robert Widdemere, it is time that we were returning, for even before we left, the turkey had gone into the oven and we must not keep Miss Dahlia waiting."

"Right you are!" the lad gaily replied as again they started down the trail, "although a month ago it would not have seemed possible, I am truly ravenously hungry."

Down the mountain road they went, these two who so enjoyed each other's companionship, little dreaming who they would find at the end of the trail.

CHAPTER XV.
SUDDEN CHANGES.

Leaving their ponies at the stables, the two hand in hand walked along the path in the glowing garden. "I'm glad the yellow crysanthemums are at their loveliest now," the girl cried. "I'm going to gather an armful to put on the table that we may have one more thing to be thankful for."

"Good, I'll help you!" the boy broke a curling-petaled beauty. "Nan, these shall be our friendship flowers. They seem so like you, so bright and colorful; joyful within themselves, and radiating it on all who pass."

When the girl's arms were heaped with the big curling, glowing blossoms, the lad suddenly cried; "Lady Red Bird, I completely forgot something very important."

"What?" the girl turned toward him to inquire.

"This!" he took from his pocket a folding kodak, "I wanted to take a picture of you at the top of the trail and I never thought of it until now. Please stand still, there, just where you are, with the fountain back of you and the crysanthemums all around you. Don't look so serious, Nan. Laugh won't you? There, I snapped it and you had not even smiled. You had such a sad far away look. What were you thinking."

"I just happened to think of Little Tirol and how I hope it is all true, that there is a God to care for him and give him another body, one without pain."

"Dear sister," the boy said, "you do have such strange and unexpected thoughts. How did you happen to think of Little Tirol now?"

"Perhaps it was because I remembered that day only two months ago, when he and I first came to the garden. The yellow flowers were just beginning to bloom and I wanted one so. I hoped he knows now that I can gather them, a great armful if I wish." Then the girl skipped toward the house, as she called merrily: "If you were ravenously hungry on the mountain trail, what must you be now, I hope we are not late."

"There is someone watching us from a front window," the boy said. "I saw a curtain move. Miss Dahlia would not do that, would she, Nan?"

"I hardly think so. It was probably the maid; though I can't think what she would be doing in the front room when it must be almost time to serve dinner."

Robert Widdemere paused a moment at the vine hung outside portal to speak with an old gardener whom he had known since his little boyhood. Nan, singing her joyous bird song without words, climbed the stairs to the library and before she had reached the door she called happily, "Oh Miss Dahlia, Robert Widdemere and I have had such a glorious ride up the mountain road, and too, we climbed to the very summit. Isn't it wonderful—" she got no farther, for having entered the library she realized that the fashionably dressed stranger standing there was not the little woman whom she so loved.

"Oh, pardon me!" the gypsy girl said. "I thought you were Miss Dahlia."

"Here I am, dearie," a trembling voice called as that little lady appeared from the dinning room. "I was needed for one moment in the kitchen," she explained, then turning toward the stranger she said almost defiantly, "Mrs. Widdemere, this is my dearly loved protege, Nan Barrington. Nan, Robert's mother has returned unexpectedly from France."

"Yes, and at great inconvenience to myself, I can assure you, to forbid my son associating with a common gypsy girl."

Miss Dahlia drew herself up proudly, and never before had she so closely resembled Miss Ursula.

"Mrs. Widdemere," she said, "kindly remember that you are in my home, and that you are speaking of my protege."

At that moment Robert appeared and was puzzled to see Miss Dahlia standing with a protecting arm about Nan, and the proud angry tone of her voice, he had never before heard. Then he saw the other woman with a sneering smile on her vain, pretty face, and he understood all.

"Mother," he said, "did you not receive the message that I sent you? Did I not tell you that you need not return to the States, that my health was recovered?"

"Yes," Mrs. Widdemere replied coldly, "and now I understand why you did not return to the school where I had placed you. You, a Widdemere, neglecting your education that you might associate with one of a class far beneath you; but I forbid you, from this day, ever again speaking to this gypsy girl."

Nan's eyes flashed, but she replied proudly, "Mrs. Widdemere, you do not need to command. I myself shall never again speak to one of your kind," then turning, she left the library.

A few moments later, when Robert and his mother were gone, Miss Dahlia went to the girl's room and found her lying on her bed sobbing as though her heart would break.

"You see, Miss Dahlia," she said, "there's no use trying to make a lady of me. I'm merely a gypsy and I'll only bring sorrow to you."

The little woman sat by the couch and tenderly smoothing the dark hair, she said: "Little girl, you are all I have to love in the world. My sister is too occupied with many things to be my companion. It grieves me deeply to have you so hurt, but I have thought out a plan, dearie, by which this may all be prevented in the future. Tomorrow morning, early, you and I are going away to a little town in the East which was my childhood home."

Nan's sobs grew less and she passionately kissed the hand that carressed her. The little lady continued:—"I will legally adopt you, and then, truly, will your name be Nan Barrington. After that I am going to send you to the Pine Crest Seminary, which is conducted by a dear schoolmate of mine, Mrs. Dorsey. I want you to permit me to select your wardrobe, which shall be like that of other girls, and no one there will dream that you are a gypsy, for many there are who have dark hair and eyes and an olive complexion. Will you do all this for me, Nan darling, because I love you?"

Nan's arms were about the little woman as she said, "How good you are to me, how kind! I'll try again to be a lady for your sake, and I hope that in time I'll be able to repay you for all that you do for me."

That afternoon was spent in packing and the next morning, soon after sunrise, Miss Dahlia and Nan were driven away, but they did not leave a forwarding address.

Robert Widdemere lifted the heavy iron knocker of the Barrington home about nine o'clock. He wanted to ask Miss Dahlia's pardon, and to tell Nan, that although he was about to return to the Military Academy to please his mother, he would never forget the promise he had made on the mountain, that he would always be her brother and her friend.

When Robert learned that Nan was gone and that he had no way of communicating with her, he felt that again a great loss had come into his life.

CHAPTER XVI.

SCHOOL GIRLS.

Several years have passed since that day in California when Nan Barrington and Robert Widdemere had parted so sadly and neither had heard ought of the other in all that time.

Nan, in a home-like girls' school near Boston, The Pine Crest Seminary, had blossomed into as charming a young lady as even Miss Ursula could desire, and that proud woman, who had changed little with the years, often gazed at the beautiful dark girl, silently wondering if it might be possible that Nan was not a real gypsy after all.

True to her promise to the dear Miss Dahlia, Nan had worn quiet colors like the other gorigo maidens, and, during the three and a half years that she had been at the school, nothing had occurred that would even suggest the roving life of her childhood, but unfortunately an hour was approaching when that suspicion would be aroused.

The Miss Barringtons remained during the winter months in Boston, but they frequently visited the school, and, during the summer, they took Nan with them to their cabin on the rocky and picturesque coast of Maine.

One Saturday afternoon Miss Dahlia was seated in the little reception room at the school and a maid had gone in search of the girl. First she referred to a chart in the corridor, which told where each of the forty pupils should be at that hour, and then, going to the music room, she tapped on the door. The sweet strains of a harp drifted out to her, and she tapped again.

"Come in," a singing voice called, and the door opened.

"Miss Nan, it's your aunt, Miss Barrington, who is waiting to see you."

"Oh, I thank you, Marie!" the happy girl exclaimed, then, springing up from the seat by her beautiful golden instrument, she said happily to the friend who was standing near: "Phyllis do come with me and meet my Aunt. I am always telling her about you, but you have been so occupied with one task or another that I have never had the opportunity to have you two meet each other."

Then as she covered her harp, she continued: "My Aunt Dahlia believes you to be as beautiful as a nymph and as joyous as a lark." Then whirling and catching both hands of her friend, Nan cried, "And when Aunt Dahlia really sees you, what do you suppose she will think?"

"That I'm a frumpy old grumpy, I suppose," Phyllis laughingly replied.

"Indeed not!" Nan declared. "You're the most beautiful creature that Nature ever fashioned with sunshine for hair, bits of June sky for eyes, the grace of a lily and—"

"Nan, do stop! I'll think that you are making fun of me, and all this time your Aunt Dahlia waits above. Come let us go. I am eager to meet her." These two girls had been room-mates and most intimate friends since Phyllis came to the school at the beginning of the year.

No two girls could be more unlike as Nan had said. She was like October night, and her friend was like a glad June day.

"Aunt Dahlia, dearie," Nan exclaimed a few moments later, as she embraced the older lady, "here at last is my room-mate, Phyllis. You are the two whom I most love, and I have so wanted you to know each other."

"And you look just exactly as I knew you would from all our Nan has told me about you. Just as sweet and pretty."

Miss Dahlia's kind face did not reveal that she was even a day older than she had been that Thanksgiving nearly four years before.

Nan asked about Miss Barrington, the elder and was told, that, as usual, she was busy with clubs of many kinds. "We are very unlike, my sister, and I," the little lady explained to Phyllis, "I like a quiet home life, Ursula is never happier than when she is addressing a large audience of women, and it does not in the least fluster her if there are men among them, on weighty questions of the day. Yes, we are very unlike."

"I am glad that you are." Nan nestled lovingly close to the little old lady. "Not but that I greatly admire and truly do care for Aunt Ursula. She has been very kind to me since she began to like me." Nan laughed, then stopped as though she had been about to say something she ought not, as indeed she had been. She had nearly said that her Aunt Ursula had started to really like her when she felt that the girl had been properly civilized and Christianized, for, ever since the talk she had had with Robert Widdemere, Nan had really tried in every way to accept the religion of the gorigo.

"Aunt Dahlia," she suddenly exclaimed, "what do you suppose is going to happen? The music master has offered a medal of gold to the one of us whose rendering of a certain piece, which he has selected, shall please him the most at our coming recital. Phyllis is trying for it on the violin; Muriel Metcalf and I on the harp, and Esther Willis on the piano. I do hope you and Aunt Ursula will be able to come."

"Nothing but illness could keep me away," Miss Dahlia said as she rose to go.

CHAPTER XVII.

OLD MEMORIES REVIVED.

The two girls with arms about each other stood on the front veranda watching as Miss Dahlia was being driven along the circling drive. Nan knew that she would turn and wave at the gate. A moment later she saw the fluttering of a small white handkerchief. The girls waved their hands, then turned indoors and climbed the wide, softly carpeted stairway and entered the room which they shared together.

It was a strange room for each girl had decked her half of it as best suited her taste. On one side the birds' eye maple furniture was made even daintier with blue and white ruffled coverings. There was a crinkly blue and white bedspread with pillow shams to match, while on the dresser there was an array of dainty ivory and blue toilet articles, two ivory frames containing the photographs of Phyllis' father and mother, and a small book bound in blue leather in which she wrote the events of every day. There were a few forget-me-nots in a slender, silver glass vase, and indeed, everything on that side of the room suggested the dainty little maid who occupied it.

But very unlike was the side occupied by the gypsy girl. Boughs of pine with the cones on were banked in one corner. Her toilet set was ebony showing off startlingly on the bureau cover which was a glowing red.

There were photographs of Aunt Dahlia and Aunt Ursula in silver band frames, gifts to her from the aunts themselves, but on the walls there were pictures of wild canon places, long grey roads that seemed to lure one to follow, pools in quiet meadowy places, and a printed poem beginning—

"Oh, to be free as the wind is free!

The vagabond life is the life for me."

But the crowning touch was the gorgeous crimson and gold shawl with its long fringe mingled with black threads that was spread over her bed. Every girl who came into their room admired it, many asked questions about how it came into Nan's possession, but to one and all the gypsy girl gave some laughing reply, and as each and every explanation was different, they knew that she was inventing stories to amuse them. Indeed, Nan was often called upon, when storms kept the girls within doors, to invent tales for their entertainment as they sat about the great stone fireplace in the recreation hall, and the more thrilling the tales were, the more pleased her audience. Sometimes Nan recalled another group, to whom she had, in the long ago, so often told stories. Little dark, fox-like creatures with their unkempt hair hanging about their faces. How eagerly they had followed Nan's every word. Poor little neglected things! Nan often longed to be able to do something for them all, to give them a chance to make something of themselves as she had been given a chance.

But would they want it? Had she not rebelled at first when Miss Ursula tried to civilize and Christianize her?

Having entered their room, the gypsy girl went at once to the wide window and looked out across the school grounds where the trees and shrubs were still leafless. "Dearie," she said, "Spring is in the air and calling us to come out. I don't want to practice now. Suppose we climb to the top of Little Pine Hill that looks down on the highway."

"But I ought to study my French verbs." Phyllis hesitated —

"French verbs on Saturday?" Nan protested, "When a merry breeze waits to run us a race!"

The fair maiden laughingly donned her wraps and a few moments later these two were tramping across the fields, and then more slowly they began climbing the path that led over the little hill.

There they stood side by side gazing down at the winding highway which, a short distance beyond, was entirely hidden by a bend and a massing of great old pines.

"Aren't bends in the road interesting?" Nan said. "One never knows what may appear next. Let's guess what it will be, and see who is nearest right."

"Very well," Phyllis replied, "I'll guess that it's the little Wharton girl out horse-back riding with her escort. She passes almost every afternoon at about this hour."

"And I'll guess that it will be a motoring party from Boston in a handsome limousine," Nan replied. Then hand in hand these two girls stood intently watching the bend in the road.

Several moments passed and Nan's attention had been attracted skyward by the flight of a bird, when she heard Phyllis' astonished exclamation: "We were both wrong, Nan! Will you look? I never saw such a queer equipage as the one which is coming. A covered wagon drawn by black horses and there is another following it and still another. How very curious! Did you ever see anything like it?"

Phyllis was so intently watching the approaching wagons that she did not notice the almost frightened expression that had appeared in the dark eyes of the girl she so loved, but after a moment Nan was able to say quite calmly, "Why, yes, Joy, I have seen a gypsy caravan before. In California where it is always summer, they often pass the Barrington home in San Seritos."

Then she added, "I'm going back to the school now."

Her friend looked at her anxiously, "Why dear," she said, "do you feel faint or ill?"

Nan shook her head and remarked lightly, with an attempt at gaiety: "Maybe my conscience is troubling me because I'm keeping you from the French verbs."

They returned to the school, and although Phyllis said nothing, she was convinced that the sight of the gypsy caravan had in some way affected Nan.

The truth was that the gypsy girl's emotions had been varied and conflicting. Her first impulse had been to run and hide, as though she feared that she might be discovered and claimed, but, a second thought assured her that this could not be the caravan of Queen Mizella and her cruel son Anselo Spico, for had she not left them in far-away California?

And yet, as she gazed intently at the wagon in the lead, again came the chilling thought that it was strangely familiar, and then she recalled a memoried picture of one evening around the camp fire when Anselo had expressed a desire to some day return to Rumania, and, to do so, they would have to come to the Eastern States.

Then another emotion rushed to the heart of the watching girl. She remembered with tenderness the long years of loving devotion that Manna Lou had given her. She wondered if that kind gypsy woman had missed her when she ran away. Tears rushed to her eyes as she thought how selfish she had been. She should have tried long ago to let Manna Lou know that all was well with her.

Then it was that Nan decided to go close to the highway, and, from a hiding place watch the caravan as it passed, but she wanted to go alone. If it should be the band of Queen Mizella, then Nan would try in some way to communicate with Manna Lou.

With this determination in her heart, she had suggested to return to school. Phyllis who was really glad to have an opportunity to study her French verbs, went back willingly, but she glanced often at the dark face of the friend she so loved. She could not understand why Nan had suddenly lost her merry mood and had become so quiet and thoughtful.

Luckily for the gypsy girl's plan, the French teacher, Madame Reznor, delayed Phyllis in the lower corridor, and Nan, leaving them, hurried to her room. Taking from the closet a long, dark cloak with a hood-cape, she slipped it on, and looking cautiously about the upper corridor to be sure that she was unobserved, she tripped lightly down the back stairs and out at the basement door.

She heard a gong ringing in the school, and she was glad, for it was calling all the pupils to the study hall, and there would be no one to spy upon her actions. But she was mistaken, for two of the girls who had been for a cross-country hike were returning, and one of them, Muriel Metcalf, chanced to glance in that direction just as Nan crouched behind the hedge that bordered the school grounds on the highway.

"Daisy Wells," Muriel exclaimed, "how queerly Nan Barrington is acting. Let's watch her and see what she is going to do."

This they did, standing behind a spreading pine tree.

CHAPTER XVIII.

A GYPSY CAMP.

Several moments Nan Barrington waited crouching behind the hedge, but the caravan did not come, nor did she hear the rattle and rumble of approaching wagons. Perhaps after all they had passed while she was indoors. Disappointed, the girl arose, and was about to return to the school when she heard voices that seemed to come from a small grove beyond the seminary grounds. Hurrying along in the shelter of the hedge, Nan reached a small side gate, and, hidden, she looked up the highway.

She saw that the gypsies had drawn to one side of the road and were preparing to make camp for the night. They were so near that she could plainly hear what they were saying and see the faces that were strange to her.

Muriel Metcalf and Daisy Wells were more puzzled than before.

"What do you suppose it is that Nan sees?" Muriel whispered. "She surely is much excited about something. Come, let's run to the tree that's nearest the hedge and then we will know."

This they did, watching Nan intently, to be sure that they were not observed, but the gypsy girl looked only at the camp wondering what she should do. At last, assured that she had nothing to fear, and longing, if possible, to hear some word of Manna Lou, who had mothered her through the first fourteen years of her life, she drew her cloak more closely about her, and, opening the gate, she went over to the camp fire.

How familiar it all seemed. There were the same little fox-like children scampering about gathering wood, and tears rushed to Nan's eyes as she remembered, how in the long ago, those other children had always run to meet her with arms outstretched when she returned to camp on her Binnie, but these children paid her little heed, for often fine young ladies come to have their fortunes told.

A kindly-faced gypsy woman, who was bending over the fire, looked up as she said, "Ah, pretty leicheen, have you come to cross my palm with silver? A wonderful future awaits you, dearie. I can tell that from your eyes."

Then to the amazement of all within hearing, Nan replied in the Romany language. The gypsy woman held out her arms with evident joy as she said in her own tongue, "So, pretty leicheen, you are one of us! Tell me, dearie, how did it happen? Was your mother a gypsy and your father, perhaps a gorigo?"

"My mother was a gypsy," the girl replied, "but she has long been dead and I have been adopted by a kind gorigo lady, two of them, and I am attending this school."

Other gypsy women gathered about and they urged Nan to remain with them for the evening meal, but she said that she would be missed from the school if she were not there for dinner.

"But there is much that I want to ask you," the girl said, "and if I possibly can, I will return after dark."

"Come, come, dearie leicheen," the gypsy women urged, "We will be glad to have you."

Then, as it was late, Nan hurried away. The twilight was deepening and though she passed close to their hiding place, she did not see the two girls who had been spying upon her.

When she was gone, Muriel exclaimed, "Daisy Wells, did you hear her? She spoke the gypsy language."

"Yes," her friend replied. "I have always thought that there was something strange about Nan Barrington and now I know what it is. She is a gypsy."

"If that is true, one of us will leave this school," Muriel said haughtily, "for my mother would not permit me to associate with a common gypsy."

CHAPTER XIX.

AN ENEMY.

During the dinner hour Phyllis glanced often at her dearest friend wondering, almost troubled, at the change that had so recently come over her. Across the wide refectory, two other pairs of eyes were also watching Nan and in the proud face of Muriel Metcalf there was a sneering expression.

"How guilty Nan Barrington acts," she said softly to the girl at her side.

"She dreads having the truth found out, I suppose," Daisy Wells replied, "but probably we are the only ones who know it and of course we would not tell."

Muriel's pale blue eyes turned toward her friend and her brows were lifted questioningly, as she inquired:—"Indeed? Who said that we would not tell?"

"I will not," Daisy replied quietly. "My mother has told me to ask myself two questions before repeating something that might hurt another. First, is it kind; second, is it necessary? So, Muriel, why tell, since it is neither kind nor necessary?"

Daisy's natural impulses were always good, but she often seemed to be easily led by her less conscientious friend, Muriel Metcalf.

"Oh well, you may side with her if you prefer," the other said with a shrug of her shoulders, "but I shall watch her closely tonight and see what she does. I wouldn't be a bit surprised if she went back to the gypsy camp, and, as for telling, I shall do as I think best about that."

To herself Muriel added, "If Nan Barrington wins the gold medal at the recital contest next Saturday, it shall be known all over the school before night that she is only a gypsy." Wisely, she said nothing of this to Daisy Wells, whose sense of justice, she knew, would scorn such an act of jealousy.

Nan was planning, as soon as she left the dining hall, to go at once to the office of Mrs. Dorsey and ask permission to go out of grounds, and, since she was an honor student, she knew the request would be granted without question. As the girls were sauntering through the corridors after dinner in groups of two and three, Phyllis exclaimed: —

"Well, Nan dear, the wonderful night has arrived at last," and then when her friend's dark eyes were turned toward her questioningly, she added merrily, "Nan Barrington, do you mean to tell me that you have forgotten what we are to do tonight? Why only this morning you said how glad you were that the day had at last arrived."

Then it was that Nan recalled the long-planned and much-anticipated theatre party. Madame Reznor was to chaperone her class in dramatics that they might see a noted actor in a Shakespearian play which they were studying.

Since the appearance of the gypsy caravan, she had forgotten all else.

What should she do? Nan, who had never told a lie, could not say that she was ill or that she did not want to go.

"Come, dear," Phyllis was saying, "I will help you dress as we are to start in half an hour. The rest of us dressed before dinner, but though I hunted everywhere, I could not find you."

Nan permitted herself to be led to their room and mechanically she let down her long dark hair. Suddenly the thought came to her that she would awaken at dawn and slip out to the camp and then she could ask her gypsy friends if they knew aught of her Manna Lou.

Half an hour later, trying to assume a spirit of merriment that she might not mar the joyousness of the others, Nan climbed into the waiting car that was to take them to the city. Muriel watched her go, then turning to Daisy Wells, she said, "Now, you and I are going down to the gypsy camp and find out what it was that Nan Barrington said when she was talking in that queer language."

The other girl looked up from the problem that she was trying to solve, as she replied, "No Muriel, I am not going. I promised little Janet that I would help her with her sums tonight. She has been ill and is eager to catch up with her class, and, moreover, I have no desire to spy upon actions of a schoolmate."

"Oh, indeed!" Muriel said with a toss of her head and then she added sarcastically, "Aren't you afraid that you will soon be sprouting wings? It seems to me that you have become a saint very suddenly."

Daisy had arisen and was gathering up her books and papers as she quietly replied, "No, Muriel, I am not pretending to be better than anyone else, but I like Nan Barrington, no one could help liking her, she is so kind and generous, and I do not in the least care what her ancestry may be. Yes, Janet dear, I'm coming right away," she added to the frail little girl who had appeared in the doorway.

Muriel, left alone, put on a long cloak, and, winding a scarf about her head, she went out. Well she knew that it was against the rules to go beyond the seminary grounds at night, but she did not care. Something was all wrong in the heart of Muriel Metcalf, and that something was jealousy which was rapidly becoming hatred. She had so wanted to win the medal of gold, but she knew that Nan Barrington had practiced far more conscientiously. Vaguely Muriel thought that, perhaps, if she could find out something against Nan, she might have her barred from the coming contest.

Having reached the gate in the hedge, Muriel peered through, and saw, in the light of the camp fire, the gypsies sitting close about it, for the night was cold. When the girl approached, one of the gypsy women rose and called in greeting, "Ha, pretty leicheen, I feared you were not coming." Then, as the firelight fell on the face of the girl, she added truly disappointed, "but you are not the same. Could she not come, the other little girl?"

"No," Muriel replied. "She wished me to say that she had to go into the city." Then eager to obtain the information for which she had come, she added hurriedly, "Nan Barrington tells me that she too, is a gypsy."

"Yes, the pretty leicheen is one of us." Then, in a wheedling voice, the gypsy woman said, "Let me tell your fortune, dearie. Cross my palm with silver. I see much happiness for you, but it is far off. First there is trouble.

You are trying to harm someone who is your friend, someone who is to do much to help you. You should not do this."

Muriel's eyes flashed as she said haughtily. "I did not come here to have my fortune told. Thanks to you I have learned what I wished to know." Then, without another word, she walked rapidly toward the side gate, but her heart was indeed troubled; she could not understand why, or would not, and it was late before she fell asleep. Too, it was late when Phyllis and Nan Barrington returned to their room and Nan's last conscious thought was that she wanted to waken before daybreak that she might visit the gypsy camp.

CHAPTER XX.

NAN DISAPPOINTED.

In spite of her resolve to waken before dawn, Nan did not open her eyes until the sunlight was flooding in at the wide bow window. Springing up, she began at once to dress quietly, and then, with a last glance at Phyllis who seemed to be sleeping she left the room, but her friend had opened her eyes in time to see Nan stealing out so silently.

However, this was not unusual, for the gypsy girl, who in her childhood had always been up to greet the dawn, often went to the top of Little Pine Hill to watch the sunrise and to remember many things, and so since it was still too early to dress, Phyllis nestled back for another few moments of slumber.

Meanwhile Nan, with the dark cloak wrapped snugly about her, for the morning air was tinglingly cold, hurried across the wide grounds and down to the hedge near the highway, but she paused at the gate and gazed, not at the caravan as she had hoped, but at the charred remains of the camp fire.

Her gypsy friends were gone! Truly disappointed, she was about to return when she saw something white pinned to a great pine tree, and wondering what it could be, she slipped through the gate and looked at it more closely. It was a piece of folded wrapping paper addressed to "The Pretty Leicheen." She was sure that it was intended for her. The kind gypsy woman had left some message. Opening it, she read: "We could not wait, dearie. We must be in the next town by noon. A girl from the school came to us last night. She tries to harm you. If you are not happy, come to us. We will be there until tomorrow, Queen Luella."

Nan folded the paper again and placed it in her pocket. Then she stood looking down the highway, shining in the sun, and there were many emotions in her heart, but she was most conscious of a loneliness, for once more she had lost a possible opportunity of hearing about her dear Manna Lou. If only she had Binnie, she could gallop after the caravan and soon overtake it, but the pony, that had been her comrade in those other days, was still at San Seritos. Then, with a sigh, she turned back and slowly crossed the school grounds.

Happening to slip her hand into the pocket of her coat, she touched the folded paper and then she remembered the message that it contained. What could Queen Luella have meant? She, Nan Barrington, had an enemy? Nan wished harm to no one and she always tried to be kind, then why should there be someone wishing to harm her?

"Well, early bird," Phyllis sang out as Nan entered their room, "what did you capture this morning? Wet feet, for one thing."

"Right you are," the gypsy girl gaily replied as she threw off the long wrap and sat on a low stool to change her shoes. The cloak fell over a chair and from the pocket a paper fluttered to the floor near Phyllis.

Nan hurriedly reached for it and tearing it into small bits, she tossed the pieces into a waste basket. Her friend was indeed puzzled. It was so unlike her room-mate to have secrets. What could it all mean? She wondered as she gazed into the mirror and brushed her long, sunlit hair.

Phyllis felt a desire to go to her friend and put her arms about her and beg to be allowed to help if anything had gone wrong, but she did not for she well knew that Nan would tell her if it were something that she wished to share.

The gypsy girl said suddenly after several moments of deep thought, "do you think that I have an enemy in this school?"

"An enemy? You, Nan? No indeed! Everyone loves you! How could they help it? You are always doing nice things for the girls and I never heard you say an unkind word about anyone, so how could you have an enemy?" Phyllis was amazed at the suggestion.

Nan rose and laughingly embraced her friend. "Well," she merrily declared, "it is quite evident that you, at least, are not that enemy. Don't think anything more about it. I was sure that I did not have one. Good! There's the breakfast bell." But, try as she might to forget, she could not, and during the morning meal, Nan's glance roamed from one face to another as she wondered who among the pupils of Pine Crest Seminary had, the night before, visited the gypsy camp.

CHAPTER XXI.

THE POWER OF LOVING-KINDNESS.

The next afternoon at four, Nan went down to the music room as it was her hour to practice on the harp, Muriel Metcalf having been there the hour preceding. Before opening the door, Nan listened to be sure that the other young harpist had finished, and, as she heard no sound within, she decided that Muriel had gone, but, upon opening the door, she saw the other girl seated by a table, her head on her arms and her shoulders shaken with sobs.

Muriel sprang up when she heard the door close and in her pale blue eyes there was an expression of hatred when she saw who had entered the room.

"Dear, what has happened?" Nan Barrington exclaimed with her ever-ready sympathy. Then, putting a loving arm about the girl, she added: "Is there something that I can do to help?"

"No, there isn't!" Muriel flung out. "You'll probably be glad when you hear what has happened. That horrid old Professor Bentz told me that if I did not have this week's lesson perfect, he would no longer teach me on the harp. I suppose I am stupid, but I just can't, can't get it, and tomorrow is the day that he comes. I wouldn't care for myself, but my father will be heart-broken. He had a little sister, who played on the harp, and she died. Dad just idolized her, the way he does me. He kept the harp and he is so eager to have me play upon it. I just can't bear to disappoint him." For the moment Muriel seemed to have forgotten to whom she was talking.

"Nor shall you," Nan said quietly. "Is this your free hour, Muriel?"

"Yes," was the reply. "Why?"

"I thought perhaps you would like to stay while I practice. Our lesson is hard this week, but I might be able to help you. Would you like to stay?"

Muriel hardly knew how to reply. Judging others by her own selfish standard, she had supposed that Nan would be glad if she were barred from the coming recital, but instead, the gypsy girl was offering to help her master that part which had seemed to her most difficult.

"Thank you, I will stay," she heard herself saying, and then she sat quietly near while Nan played the lesson through from beginning to the end. "Now, Muriel," the harpist said, with her friendly smile, "will you play it for me, and then I can better tell which part is your stumbling block?"

Patiently Nan showed the other girl how to correct her mistakes, until, at length, a gong rang in the corridor calling them to the study hall.

Springing up, the gypsy girl exclaimed: "You did splendidly, Muriel! If I could help you just once more before your lesson, I think that Professor Bentz would have no fault to find with you." Then she added kindly, "You really have talent, dear, but you haven't practiced very faithfully of late. If you wish, I will come with you to the music room this evening during our recreation hour and we can go over it once again."

"Thank you! I would like to come," Muriel replied, but oh, what a strangely troubled feeling there was in her heart as she remembered the words of the gypsy woman: "You are trying to harm someone, who will do much to help you."

That evening at 7 o'clock the two girls were again in the music room and Muriel played the piece through so well that Nan exclaimed with real enthusiasm, "Dearie, you did that beautifully, especially the part where it seems as though a restless spirit is yearning to be forgiven for something. Really, Muriel, the tears came into my eyes, for you played it with true feeling."

Then to the gypsy girl's surprise the little harpist began to sob.

"Oh, Nan, I do want to be forgiven for something. You've been so kind to help me and I've been so horrid and mean to you."

"Why, Muriel, you have never been horrid or mean to me."

"Oh, yes, I have. Only yesterday I was planning to do something that I thought would turn the girls all against you. I was jealous, I suppose, because Professor Bentz always holds you up as a model. Then I overheard you talking to the gypsies and that night I visited their camp and found out that you were one of them, and so I decided that if you won the gold medal I would tell every one in the school about it. There now, don't you call that being mean and horrid?"

Nan's joyous laugh rang out, and she gaily exclaimed: — "Oho, so you are the enemy I have been looking for?" Then she added, with sudden seriousness: "My dear Muriel, I am not ashamed because I am a gypsy, and I would gladly have proclaimed it from the top of Little Pine Hill if I had not promised Miss Barrington that I would not."

"And you're going to forgive me?" Muriel asked, although she knew the answer before it was spoken.

"There is nothing to forgive. Hark! Someone is coming. Who do you suppose that it is?"

There was a merry rapping on the door, and then it was opened, revealing two maidens. There was an expression of surprise on the pretty face of the younger girl, but it was Phyllis who exclaimed, "Well, Nan, here you are. I have hunted for you high and low. I just met Daisy in the corridor and she was searching for Muriel." Then, glancing from one expressive face to the other, she added: "What has happened? You girls look as though you had a secret."

"So we have," Nan laughingly replied. "I was just going to tell Muriel a story and if you girls will come in and be seated, you too, may hear it."

Phyllis, wondering what it all might mean, listened with increasing interest as Nan told about the caravan of Queen Mizella and about the loving kindness of Manna Lou to the little crippled boy, Tirol, and to the little orphan girl whose mother had died so long ago.

"I didn't know that there were such good, unselfish women among the gypsies," Phyllis declared, "but, Nan, why are you telling us this story?"

"Because I am the orphaned girl," was the quiet reply.

"You!" Phyllis exclaimed. "Now I know why you are so wonderful and why you seem to understand the songs of the birds and feel such a comradeship for the trees and sky and all out-of-doors."

"Then you don't love me any the less?" the question was asked in half seriousness.

"Nan, what do I care who your ancestors are?" Phyllis declared. "It is you whom I love."

"Hark!" the gypsy girl said with lifted finger. "The chapel bell is calling us to evening prayer." And then, as she and Muriel were the last to leave the room, she kissed the younger girl as she whispered, "Good night, dear little friend."

CHAPTER XXII.

THE CONTEST RECITAL.

The day of the contest dawned gloriously. During the night pink and golden crocuses had blossomed on the seminary grounds and each bush and tree was a haze of silvery green.

In the mid-afternoon two girls stood at an open library window. They were Muriel and Nan and they were waiting their turn at the recital. In the study hall beyond many parents and friends were gathered and with the teachers and pupils of the seminary, they were listening with pride and pleasure to the rendering of solos on violin and piano, while at one side of the platform, a golden harp stood waiting.

"Daisy Wells is playing now," Muriel said, "Are you nervous Nan?"

"No dearie." Then the older girl exclaimed joyfully, "Do look in the lilac bush! The first robin has come, and now he is going to sing for us. He surely would win the medal if he were to enter the contest."

Muriel looked up at the other maiden and slipping an arm about her, she said impulsively, "I love you."

Then, before the gypsy girl could reply, the younger harpist was called. "Oh Nan," she said in a sudden panic of fear.

"Think of your father, dearie and just play for him." How calming that suggestion had been, and, while she played, Muriel was thinking of the twilight hours when her father had lifted her to his knee, and, holding her close, had told her of that other little girl whom he had so loved, and how lonely his boyhood had been when that little sister had died, and, how like her, Muriel was. "It will be a happy day for me, little daughter, when I hear you play as she did on the harp," he had often said.

When the last sweet notes were stilled, there were tears in many eyes, for Muriel, forgetting all others, had played alone for her father.

Professor Bentz was amazed and delighted. "I knew she had talent," he said to Mrs. Dorsey, the principal of the school, "but I did not know that she could play like that."

When the recital was over, it was to Muriel that the medal of gold was awarded.

"Oh Nan, I ought not to take it. You have done it all!"

There was a happy light in the eyes of the gypsy girl as she stooped and kissed her little friend. "You played wonderfully dearie!" she said.

Just at that moment a maid appeared in the library door, where the performers had gathered. "Miss Muriel," she called, "there is a gentleman here to see you."

"It's father!" the little girl cried with eyes aglow. "I do believe that he came for the recital."

And she was right. Mr. Metcalf was standing in the small reception room and he caught his little daughter in his arms and held her close for a moment without speaking.

He said in a choking voice: "My dream is fulfilled. You play the harp, Muriel, as my sister did."

Then he told her that he had long planned to visit her at the school and had timed that visit so that he might be present at the recital without her knowing it.

"I think I must have known it, somehow," the happy little girl said, "for I was playing only for you."

And Nan Barrington, who had done so much to help Muriel, felt that the winning of the love of her little "enemy" was far more to be desired than the winning of the medal of gold.

CHAPTER XXIII.

A JOYOUS INVITATION.

A month had passed and the orchard back of the school was a bower of pink and white blooms, while oriole, robin and meadow lark made the fragrant sunlit air joyous with song.

Gypsy Nan stood at the open window of their room gazing out over the treetops to the highway, and how she yearned for her pony Binnie. She longed to gallop away, away—where, she cared little. Then she thought of the happy ride she and Robert Widdemere had taken three years before, and, sitting down on the window seat, with her chin resting on one hand, she fell to musing of those other days. Again she was a little girl, clad in a cherry red dress and seated in the boughs of the far-away pepper tree which stood on the edge of the Barrington estate in San Seritos. She recalled the sad, pale invalid boy in the wheeled chair, and she smiled as she remembered his surprise when a cluster of pepper berries had dropped on his listlessly folded hands. What splendid friends those two became the weeks that followed, and then there had been that last morning on the mountain top when he had promised that he would always be her friend, come what might. Little had they dreamed that years would pass, and that neither would know what had become of the other.

How she would like to see Robert Widdemere. He would be taller and broader, with a dignity of carriage which he surely would have acquired after three years' training in a military academy. How good looking he had been that long ago Thanksgiving morning when he had worn the gypsy costume!

At this point Nan's revery was interrupted by Phyllis, who fairly danced into the room. She held an open letter and she gaily exclaimed:

"Nan darling, you never could guess what you and I are going to do."

"It must be a happy something, by the way you are shining."

"Oh, it is the most exciting thing that ever happened in all my life," the other girl exclaimed joyously as she sat on the window seat facing her friend. "It's an invitation that came in this letter, and Mrs. Dorsey has granted us both permission to accept."

Nan's dark eyes were wide with wonder. "Am I invited to go somewhere?" she asked. "Please don't keep me guessing about it any longer. Do tell me where."

"Well, then, I'll have to begin at the beginning. You have often heard me speak of my cousins the Dorchesters." Nan nodded. "They have been in Florida all winter," she continued, "but now they have returned and have opened up their city home and the tenth of May will be Peggy's birthday and we are invited to her party. It will be on Saturday night, but Mrs. Dorsey said that we need not return to Pine Crest until the following day — and oh, I forgot to tell you! It's a masquerade and we must begin at once to think what costumes we will wear. I have the sweetest May Queen dress! I might wear that with a wreath of apple blossoms in my hair."

"Joy, that would just suit you, but pray what shall I wear?"

"Oh, Nan, do wear your red and gold gypsy dress. You look just beautiful in that. Say that you will to please me," Phyllis pleaded.

"Very well; to please you and also to please myself. I would just love to have an excuse to wear that wonderful shawl that once long ago belonged to my beautiful mother." There was always a wistful expression in the dark eyes when Nan spoke of the mother whom she had never known.

"Was your mother —" Phyllis hesitated.

Nan turned clear eyes toward her friend. "Was she a gypsy, do you mean? Dearie, I don't in the least mind talking about it. Ask me anything that you wish. The only part that I regret is that I cannot answer anything with real knowledge. I have always supposed that my mother was the one of my parents who was a gypsy. That is what I told Queen Luella, but afterwards, in thinking it over, I wondered if it might not have been my father, or perhaps they both belonged to the band of Queen Mizella, I was not to be told until I was eighteen."

After a thoughtful moment Phyllis ventured: "Nan, would you feel very badly if you were to discover that you are not a real gypsy at all; that perhaps your mother for some reason had given you into the keeping of Manna Lou and had died before she returned to claim you? You might have been a Rumanian princess and the throne might have been threatened and it was necessary to hide you."

Nan's merry laughter pealed out. "Phyllis, you are trying to steal my thunder, making up exciting tales as you go along. Now you know, dearie, that I have won fame, if not fortune, by improvising impossible fiction, and I do not want to relinquish, even to you, the laurels I have won."

Phyllis watching the glowing dark face asked another question. "What do the real Rumanians look like. I mean the ones that are not gypsies. Aren't they very dark and beautiful just as you are?"

Nan sprang to her feet and made a sweeping curtsy as she exclaimed dramatically: — "Would that everyone had eyes like yours. But truly, dear," the gypsy girl dropped back into her deep easy chair, "I know no more of the Rumanians than you do. Just what we have learned in our illustrated book on 'Men and Manners of Many Lands.'"

"But you haven't answered my question," the fair girl persisted. "Would you be disappointed if some day it should be discovered that you are white and —." Again Nan laughingly interrupted, making an effort to look in the mirror without rising. "Goodness, am I black?" Then, before Phyllis could remonstrate, Nan continued; "I thought I was just a nice brown or —" Her friend sprang up and kissed her lovingly, then perched on the arm of the chair, she exclaimed warmly: "You have the most velvety smooth olive complexion. Many American girls have one similar, but not nearly as nice, and now, since you do not want to answer my question, we will change the subject."

Nan, nestled lovingly against her friend. "Indeed I shall answer your question. I would be very, very sorry if I were to suddenly learn that I am not at all a gypsy. I would feel — well as though I were a stranger to myself or as though my past was a dream from which I had been rudely awakened. I wouldn't know how to begin to live as somebody quite different." Then, as a bell rang and Phyllis arose, Nan concluded: "But we need have no fear of such a sudden transforming, for I know I am a gypsy. Manna Lou never told a lie and she said time and again that the only part of my story that she would or could tell me was that I am one of their own band."

Impulsively Phyllis kissed her friend. "If being a gypsy is what makes you so adorable, I wish we had more of your band in our midst."

Then after hastily tidying and washing in their very own wee lavatory, arm in arm the two girls went down to the dining hall again, chatting happily about the week-end treat that was in store for them.

CHAPTER XXIV.

NAN'S FIRST MASQUERADE.

The home of the Dorchesters was brilliantly lighted and the little hostess Peggy, who represented a rose fairy, was exquisitely gowned in filmy pink. Her small black mask hung over her shoulder and she was arranging a huge basket of apple blossom sprays in the library when Phyllis, looking like a very lovely May Queen, entered the room.

Peggy whirled around and holding out both hands, she kissed her cousin impulsively as she exclaimed: "Oh, I'm so glad that you could come. It's just ages since I saw you last, and ever so many things have happened. Tomorrow morning we'll have a talkfast and gossip for hours, but do tell me who is the room-mate that you asked if you might bring. I just saw her a minute as you came in, but I thought that she was very beautiful, dark like a Spanish of French girl, isn't she?" Then, without waiting for an answer, impetuous Peggy hurried on as a new thought presented itself.

"Phyllis you never could guess who is coming tonight. One of our boy cousins whom we haven't seen in just ever so long, but there, I ought not to be calling him a boy, he's so big and good-looking? His mother is staying with us and she talks about her wonderful son all of the time. She plans to have him make a most eligible marriage, but he doesn't seem to care for girls at all. Oh, here comes your friend! Isn't that gypsy costume fascinating?"

Nan Barrington was presented to the little hostess and to her mother, who appeared at that moment to assist in receiving, and then the guests began to arrive.

Phyllis and Nan retreated to a seat beneath a bank of palms and not far from the hidden musicians. They had on their masks and Nan, who had never before attended a real party of any kind, was interested in all that she saw. Suddenly she caught her friend's hand as she said softly, "Phyllis, will you look at the young man who is just entering! Who do you suppose he is?"

"Why, he has on a gypsy costume! That's rather strange, isn't it? Wouldn't it be amusing, Nan, if he should ask you to dance? There are to be no personal introductions, you know. Only close friends of Aunt Lucy's and Peg's are invited, and so, of course, that in itself is sufficient introduction."

While Phyllis had been talking a youth dressed as a knight had approached and asked her to join the promenade with him, and so, for a moment Nan was left alone. She did not mind and she sat smiling as she thought how like a play it all was when suddenly she heard someone saying, "Lady Gypsy, will you promenade with me?"

Nan sprang to her feet and held out both hands impulsively:

"Robert!" she said. "I thought of you the moment that I saw that costume but it isn't the one that you wore so long ago and I never dreamed that it could be you, but your voice—I'm not mistaken in it, am I?"

For answer the lad tore off his mask and looked down at the girl with an expression of radiant joy.

"Lady Red Bird," the lad exclaimed as he led her back of the sheltering palms, "for three years I have tried and tried to find you. Did you think that I had broken the promise that I made to you high on the mountain? Indeed I have not, and I never will break it. Please remove your mask. I want to know what my sister-comrade looks like after all these years."

"Robert, I wish to speak with you." It was the voice of his mother calling softly from an open door near. The lad although deploring the interruption, was too courteous to not heed his mother's request. Hurriedly he said: "I will be back directly. I have so much to tell you and so very, very much that I want to learn about you." He was leading the gypsy girl back to her seat beneath the palm.

When he was gone Nan suddenly remembered that in her surprise and joy at finding her old-time comrade she had completely forgotten the promise that she had made his mother three years before on Thanksgiving day.

Mrs. Widdemere had then forbidden Robert to ever again speak to the gypsy girl, but before the indignant lad had time to reply, it was Nan who had said: "You need not be troubled, Mrs. Widdemere, for I shall never again speak to one of your kind."

Unconsciously she had broken that promise many times, for was not her dearly loved room-mate this woman's niece? Too, even now she had been speaking to her son. Rising, she decided that she must go away somewhere and think what would be the honorable thing for her to do, Just then she saw Phyllis approaching with her partner and, hurrying toward them, she said, "Phyllis, may I speak with you alone for a moment?"

Her friend, excusing herself, led the way into a small reception room and closed the door. "What is it, Nan? You look as though something very unusual had happened."

The gypsy girl's cheeks were burning and it was plainly evident that she was much excited. "Phyllis," she said hurriedly, "don't ask me to explain now. Please help me to get away at once. Can't I call a taxi and go to Aunt Dahlia? Something has happened and I will tell you all about it to-morrow. Don't worry dear, but I must go."

Phyllis believing that her dearest friend was about to be seriously ill, hastened to comply with her wishes. First she explained this fear to Peggy's mother, who at once called their chauffeur and directed him to take Nan to the Barrington residence.

It was not late and Miss Barrington and her younger sister. Miss Dahlia, were seated in the library reading when the girl entered. They were indeed surprised, for Nan had called on them not two hours before when she had first arrived in town.

"Dearie," Miss Dahlia exclaimed, rising and going toward the girl with outstretched hands "what is it? Are you ill?"

"No, not ill, but troubled in spirit," Nan said with a forlorn little laugh. Then she sat on a stool near the two old ladies and told all that had happened.

Miss Ursula drew herself up proudly as she said, "Sister Dahlia, why did you not tell me this before? I did not know that Anne had been so humiliated. I shall certainly inform Mrs. Widdemere that a girl whom the

Barringtons are proud to adopt as their own is quite worthy to be her son's companion. Anne, if you wish I will return with you to the party. Mrs. Dorchester and I were school-mates long ago."

"No, thank you," Nan replied rather wistfully, "I would rather not go back."

Meanwhile Robert, having left his mother, who merely wished to introduce him to an heiress, returned to find the seat beneath the palms unoccupied. Nan was gone and though he stood with folded arms and watched the passing dancers, he did not see her. At last he sought the little hostess and inquired what had become of the guest disguised as a gypsy.

CHAPTER XXV.

NAN'S DECISION.

Miss Barrington, who had learned to love Nan as dearly as had her sister, Miss Dahlia, looked admiringly at the beautiful girl, who, having removed her gypsy costume, was clad in a clinging simple white voile.

"Anne," she said, "will you play for us? The piano has not been touched in many a day."

And so Nan, always glad to please these two, played and sang the selections chosen by the elderly ladies.

Suddenly the telephone rang and a maid appeared. "Miss Barrington," she said. Nan ceased playing, and, to her surprise, she heard Miss Ursula replying to someone over the wire, "Yes indeed, you may come. We shall be glad to have you."

For some unaccountable reason Nan's heart began to beat rapidly. Could it be Robert who was coming? She wondered as she resumed her playing, but her fingers went at random and then, before it seemed possible, the door bell rang and a moment later Robert in his military uniform, entered the room.

He was gladly welcomed by the two old ladies who had known him since he wore knickerbockers and then when Nan went forward and held out her hand as she said in her frank friendly way, "Robert, forgive me for disappearing, but I suddenly remembered that I had promised your mother that I would never again speak to one of her kind, and I do sincerely wish to keep my promises."

"But, Miss Barrington," the lad appealed to the elderly woman, "should one keep a hastily made promise when there is no justice in it? I am sure that my father would approve of my friendship with Nan, and though I regret my mother's attitude, I do not think that I should be influenced by it. If you and Miss Dahlia will grant me permission to be Nan's comrade once more, I will promise to care for her as I would wish another to care for a sister of mine."

They were seated about the wide hearth for the evenings were cool.

"Robert Widdemere," Miss Ursula said, "if Anne wishes your friendship, we will welcome you into our home whenever you desire to come. We wish Anne to remain at the Pine Crest seminary until June. We are then going to our cottage on the coast of Maine until October, when we will return to San Seritos for the winter."

The lad's eyes were glowing. "How I would like to go back there," he said, then, turning to the girl, he added, laughingly, "I suppose Lady Red Bird is too grown now to climb the pepper tree."

"I suppose so," Nan replied merrily. "That is one of the penalties of being civilized."

Soon the lad rose reluctantly. "I promised Cousin Peggy that I would return for the supper dance at ten o'clock," he said, "and to keep that promise I must leave at once. But, Nan, you have not yet told me that you care to have my friendship."

The girl looked thoughtfully into the fire a moment and then replied slowly, "Robert Widdemere, I do want your friendship, but I would be happier if I might have it with your mother's consent."

"Then you shall," the boy replied.

In the meanwhile Peggy had sought Phyllis. "I don't in the least understand what is happening," she said. "First your friend, disguised as a gypsy, leaves in a panic, then Cousin Robert insists on knowing where she has gone and follows her, and when his mother heard about it, she became so angry that she went at once to her room and bade us tell Robert to come to her the moment he returns. What can it all mean?"

"It's just as much a mystery to me, Peg," Phyllis said. "But there comes Robert now. Perhaps he will explain."

The interview that Robert Widdemere had with his mother on his return from the Barrington home was not a pleasant one for either of them but in the end Robert had said firmly but gently, "I feel sure that my father would approve of my friendship with Nan and, moreover, next summer I will be

21 and I shall consider myself old enough then to choose my own companions. My dad must have expected me to possess good judgment in some degree or his request would not have been that I assume the reins of his business on my 21st birthday." Then, going to the indignant woman, he put his arm about her as he said lovingly, "Mother, dear, I want you to tell me that you are willing that I may be Nan Barrington's friend."

"It is a great disappointment," Mrs. Widdemere said, "but, since you are soon to be financially independent of me, I suppose that I might as well give my consent. However, do not expect me to receive that gypsy girl into my home as an equal, for I shall not."

The next morning Phyllis and her cousin Robert visited the Barrington home and an hour later the lad accompanied the girls to the station where they were to take the train for Pine Crest.

Robert had told Nan that he had won his mother's consent to their friendship but he did not tell how reluctantly that consent had been given.

The next day the lad returned to the Military Academy where in another month he would complete his training, but each week he and Nan exchanged letters telling of the simple though pleasant experiences of their school life.

Nan and Phyllis were to graduate in June and they were happily busy from dawn till dark. It had been the custom for many years at the Pine Crest Seminary for the pupils to make their own graduating dresses by hand. These were to be of dainty white organdie and the two girls, with their classmates, spent many pleasant hours sewing in one room and another. Tongues flew as fast as the needles while each young seamstress told what she hoped the summer and even the future would hold for her.

Nan was often thoughtfully silent these last days of school.

One twilight Phyllis found her standing alone at their open window watching the early stars come out.

"What are you thinking, dear?" she asked.

"I was wondering about my own mother," Nan replied. "Next week I will be eighteen and then it was that Manna Lou planned telling me who I am, I never could understand why she did not tell me before, but she said that she had promised, and now, that I might know, I am too far away."

"Perhaps your mother was a sister of Manna Lou," her friend suggested.

"Perhaps, but come dear," Nan added in a brighter tone, "we are due even now at French Conversation."

Nan did not speak again of the mystery of her birth, but she often wondered about it as her eighteenth birthday neared and she longed to know more of her own mother, who must have loved her so dearly.

CHAPTER XXVI.

NAN'S EIGHTEENTH BIRTHDAY.

Nan Barrington's eighteenth birthday dawned gloriously and as soon as they were dressed Phyllis disappeared to return a moment later with an armful of wonderful red roses.

"It's a happy birthday greeting from a cousin of mine," she laughingly told the surprised girl.

"Oh, are they from Peggy Dorchester?" Nan exclaimed as she took them.

Her friend's eyes twinkled. "No," she said "this cousin's name is not Peg. Guess again."

Nan's dark eyes were glowing above the beautiful bouquet. "Oh, then they are from Robert. How kind of him to remember my birthday."

Lovingly she arranged the fragrant roses in a large green jar and, selecting a bud, she placed it in her friend's belt and fastened another at her own. Then slipping her arm about Phyllis and chatting happily, they went down the broad front stairway to the refectory.

When they were returning, half an hour later, Mrs. Dorsey was in the corridor and she smiled lovingly in response to the girls' morning greeting.

"Anne," she said, "this is your eighteenth birthday, is it not? Can you spare a few moments for a visit with me?"

Nan's face brightened. "Oh yes, indeed, Mrs. Dorsey," she replied. Phyllis went on to the library and the gypsy girl entered the office with the kindly principal.

"Be seated, dear," Mrs. Dorsey said. "I have long planned having this visit with you and now that you are soon to leave us, I must no longer delay. Miss Dahlia Barrington, who, as you know, was a schoolmate of mine, told me how you chanced to come into their lives. Miss Dahlia is very proud of you and Miss Ursula is also. I, too, am proud of your splendid accomplishments, Anne. I feel that you have made much progress in the three years that you have been with us and I deeply regret that you are about to graduate. I know nothing of your plans for the future but, if the time ever comes when you wish to be self-supporting, I will be glad to give you a position as a teacher of languages and music for the younger pupils."

"Oh, Mrs. Dorsey!" Nan exclaimed gratefully, "how very kind of you to make me such an offer. If Miss Dahlia will permit me to do so, I will gladly start teaching the little ones at the beginning of the fall term. I have hoped that I might find some way to repay my benefactors, for, of course, I have been a great expense to them."

Mrs. Dorsey smiled and, as she stood, Nan also arose. "I shall indeed be glad to have you with us, Anne," the kind woman said as she kissed the girl on each cheek, then she added brightly. "Happy birthday, dear, and may each coming year find you as unspoiled and lovable as you are today."

Nan flushed happily at this praise and then she sought Phyllis to tell her the wonderful news.

"You, a teacher!" her friend cried in dismay. "Oh Nan, I did so want you to go to college with me next year. Your aunts are very rich, I am sure, and I just know that they will not think of permitting you to earn your own living."

Nan stood looking thoughtfully out of the open library window. "I would rather be independent," she declared. Then, noting her friend's dismal expression, she laughingly caught her hands as she said, "Well, we won't decide the matter, now. I'll talk it over with Aunt Dahlia when she comes."

The two girls spent a happy morning together and in the afternoon Nan said, "I wonder why Aunt Dahlia and Aunt Ursula do not come. They wrote that they would be here early and take us both for a long drive."

Another half hour passed and then there was a knock at the door.

Nan sprang up joyously. "It's Marie to tell me that my dear aunts have arrived."

It was indeed Marie, who held out a yellow envelope as she said, "This telegram just came, Miss Anne. Mrs. Dorsey isn't in, so I thought I'd better bring it right up to you."

When the door had again closed, Nan turned toward her friend with startled eyes.

"Oh Phyllis," she said fearfully, "do you suppose that Aunt Dahlia is ill?" Then, tearing open the yellow envelope, the two girls read the few words that the message contained. "Miss Ursula Barrington died last night. Miss Dahlia wishes you to come at once." The signature was that of a stranger.

"Aunt Ursula dead!" Nan repeated in dazed uncomprehension. "It can't be. It must be a mistake, for only day before yesterday I received a long letter from her and she wrote that she was feeling unusually well."

"I fear that it cannot be a mistake," her friend said tenderly, "but you must be brave and strong, Nan, for your Aunt Dahlia will need you to comfort her."

"You are right, Phyllis, I will go to her at once. Have I time to get the three o'clock train?"

"I think so, dear. You pack what we will need in your satchel and I will go and ask Patrick to bring around the school bus."

"Why, Phyllis, are you going with me? Mrs. Dorsey is not here to ask."

"I know Mrs. Dorsey would wish me to go with you. I would not think of permitting you to go alone."

A few hours later these two girls entered the city home of the Barringtons. The lower hall seemed strangely silent, and at once they ascended the stairway to Miss Dahlia's room. They found her sitting there alone and when they entered she hurried toward the girl whom she so loved. "Oh Nan darling," she said with tears rolling down her wrinkled cheeks. "I can't understand it. I can't believe that it has really happened. It was all so sudden."

The young girl held the feebled old lady in a close embrace, then leading her to a wide lounge, she sat beside her, taking the frail hands in her strong ones. "Dear Aunt Dahlia," she said, "tell me what has happened. Has Aunt Ursula been ill?"

"No, not at all. Yesterday morning a business-like looking envelope was in the mail for her. She took it at once to her study and remained there until noon, continually writing, and when at last she came to lunch, she looked worn and haggard, but when I asked her if she felt ill, she said no, and then she did something very unusual for her. She kissed me, saying in an almost pitying tone, 'Poor little sister Dahlia.'

"Directly after lunch she returned to her study and continued writing. In the afternoon she sent Dorcas to the postbox with several letters. Last night we sat by the fireplace reading when suddenly her book slipped to the floor. I looked up and saw that she seemed to be asleep. This was so very unusual that I tried to waken her, but could not.

"The doctor whom I had Dorcas summon, said that my sister must have had some great and sudden shock. What it could have been, I do not know. I searched in her desk for that business-like envelope, but it was gone."

Then leaning against the girl, she added, "Oh, Nan darling, how thankful I am that you came to us so long ago. If I did not have you, I would now be all alone in the world."

The girl kissed the little old lady tenderly as she said, "Dear Aunt Dahlia, I, too, am thankful."

Half an hour later Nan went to her own room and on her desk she saw a large envelope addressed, "To my beloved niece, Anne Barrington." The writing was Miss Ursula's.

CHAPTER XXVII.

NAN'S SUDDEN RESPONSIBILITY.

With a rapidly-beating heart Nan sat at her desk and opened the large envelope in which there was a letter and another envelope that was evidently the one to which Miss Dahlia had referred as businesslike.

"My dear Anne," the girl read, "I am prostrated with grief today and you will not wonder when I tell you that I was wrongly advised by one whom I considered a trustworthy friend, and I invested, not only my own fortune but also Sister Dahlia's in securities that I am now informed are absolutely worthless.

"I did this, I assure you, with my sister's permission, for, as you know, she had great faith in my business ability and good judgment. The result is that we are suddenly reduced to straitened circumstances which will necessitate an entire change in our mode of living.

"I am indeed glad that our Anne has been able to complete the course of studies at Pine Crest Seminary before this calamity befell us. There is one other thing which in this hour of humiliation and grief is a consolation to me, and that is that our home in San Seritos is in no way effected. It is in my sister's name and cannot be taken from her."

A blot followed and then with an evidently shaking hand had been written: "Anne, a sharp pain in my heart warns me that I must cease writing for awhile and rest. I had intended mailing this letter to you, but, remembering that it would reach you on your eighteenth birthday and shadow the happiness which is rightfully yours at that time, I have decided to place it on your desk and when you come on Sunday, you and I will retire to your room and discuss the matter.

"As you know, my dear Anne, it is difficult for me to express in words the emotions that I may feel, but I want you to know how proud I am of the little girl who came to us three years ago. You have brought a new happiness into my life and I must confess, that, though my original thought was merely to Christianize one whom I called a heathen, I myself have become more sympathetic and loving, more truly a Christian.

"Good night, Anne. If I should be taken away before my dear sister Dahlia, I will go with far greater willingness knowing that you will care for her and comfort her as long as she shall live.

"Your loving, AUNT URSULA."

The postscript had evidently been written much later. The writing was easily legible. "Anne, another of those sharp heart attacks warns me that I would better place in your care the money that we have on hand. I sent Dorcas to the bank this afternoon to draw it out and I have locked it in my desk; the key I am enclosing. There will be sufficient to care for you and sister Dahlia for at least a year; after that I am sure that my brave Anne will find a way."

Phyllis quietly entered the room a few moments later and saw Nan seated at her desk, her head on her arms.

"Oh, Phyllis," she sobbed, as her friend sat beside her and tried to comfort her, "how Aunt Ursula must have suffered. If only I had been here. Perhaps if we had talked it over together, it might have been a help to her."

Nan then gave the letter to Phyllis to read, and after a thoughtful moment, added, "I must be worthy of the trust that splendid woman has placed in me. How glad I am that I will be able to teach. I shall not tell Aunt Dahlia of the financial loss until it is necessary. She is very frail and it might be more than she could stand. Come dear, let us go to her. I do not want to leave her alone."

A week later Nan returned to Pine Crest Seminary and Miss Dahlia was with her. Mrs. Dorsey had at once visited the Barrington home and had insisted that her old friend share her pleasant apartment at the school until Nan had successfully passed the final examinations and had received her diploma.

CHAPTER XXVIII.

THE VALEDICTORIAN.

A few days before the closing exercises at Pine Crest Seminary, Phyllis entered their room and exclaimed jubilantly to the girl who was seated at the writing desk. "Nan Barrington, you never can guess who passed with the highest marks and is to be chosen class valedictorian."

The other girl looked up brightly. "It was Phyllis Dorchester, I do believe," she declared.

"No, indeed. That guess is far afield. The successful maiden is Anne Barrington. There, now, what do you think of that? Mrs. Dorsey just told me and I simply couldn't walk upstairs demurely, I was so eager to tell you. How proud I will be at the closing exercises to see my room-mate standing before a crowded assembly room reading her graduating essay on 'Comrading With Nature.' It's poetry in prose, Nan, and I am glad that you are to read it."

"But I will not be here for the closing exercises, and so if that essay is read, you will have to do it for me."

"Nan Barrington! Not be here, and the closing exercises less than a week away! Why, where are you going?"

"Sit down and I will tell you. I would love to stay, as you well know, if I had only my own wishes to consider, but each day Aunt Dahlia seems to grow more frail. Naturally Mrs. Dorsey and I have been much occupied and Aunt Dahlia has often been left alone with her sorrow in a strange apartment. Each time that I go to her, she clings to me as a frightened child would, and over and over again she tells me that she knows she will be strong again as soon as we are back in the gardens at San Seritos, then she always ends by asking in a pathetic tone, 'Nan, do you think that we will be able to go tomorrow?' and today my answer was 'yes, Aunt Dahlia, we will go tomorrow.'"

Phyllis reached for her friend's hand and held it in a sympathetic clasp and tears sprang to her eyes. She knew what a sacrifice Nan was making, for they had often talked of the happy time they would have at their graduation.

"How disappointed Robert will be," Phyllis said at last, "but, dear, of course it is right that you should go. How I do wish that I might go with you, but Mother and Dad and I are leaving for England in another month. However, if you remain in California, do not be surprised next winter to see me appearing, bag and baggage."

Nan smiled lovingly at her friend. "No one could be more welcome," she said, then she added thoughtfully, "I have indeed a difficult problem to solve for I want to live as economically as we possibly can and yet not disclose to poor Aunt Dahlia the truth concerning the lost fortune."

Phyllis sprang to her feet and kissed her friend on the forehead, as she exclaimed, "And you will be able to do it, Nan darling, I'm sure of that! Now I must depart, and you must finish that letter if it is to go on the next mail."

When Nan was alone, she continued writing until several sheets of note paper had been covered. She was telling her comrade all that had happened and explaining why she would not be able to attend her own graduating party.

Two days later the letter reached Robert Widdemere, and, after reading it, he sat for a long time gazing thoughtfully into space. In another month he would be of age and master of his own actions and possessed of a goodly income. He sprang to his feet at the call of a bugle summoning him to drill, but in his heart there was a firm resolve.

CHAPTER XXIX.

FAITHFUL FRIENDS.

A week had passed and it was nearing the end of June when Miss Dahlia and Nan arrived at the little station of San Seritos. They found Mr. Sperry, the gardener, waiting to take them home in the Barrington car, which had the family coat of arms emblazoned on the door.

Nan had written a long letter to this faithful servant and his kindly wife, telling of Miss Ursula's death and also informing them that Miss Dahlia had but little money left, and, would be obliged to dispense with the services of so expert a gardener as Mr. Sperry. Nan had then added that since Miss Dahlia was very frail, she thought best not to tell her of the changed financial conditions, but if Mr. Sperry would accept a position elsewhere, Miss Dahlia would suppose that to be the reason he was leaving her service.

When Mr. Sperry read this letter to his wife, he removed his spectacles and wiped them as he said, "Nell, Miss Dahlia is one of God's good women if there ever was one. Mind you the time little Bobsy had diphtheria and you couldn't get a nurse? You'd have died yourself with the care of it all if it hadn't been for that blessed woman coming right down here and staying quarantined in this lodge house where there weren't any comforts such as she had been used to, and now, that she's in trouble, it isn't likely we're going to desert her. No, sir, not us! The Baxters have been at me this month past to work on their place half time, and I'll do it. Then we can raise our own vegetables and plenty for Miss Dahlia besides, in the kitchen garden here and she'll never know but what Miss Nan is paying us a salary regular, just as we always had."

"You are right, Samuel," Mrs. Sperry said wiping her eyes with the corner of her blue apron. "We're not the sort to be forgetting past kindness. I'll go up to the big house this minute with Bertha and we'll air it out and have Miss Dahlia's room cheerful and waiting for her."

And so when Mr. Sperry saw Nan assisting Miss Barrington to the platform, he hurried forward, and, snatching off his cap, he took the hand the little lady held out to him. It was hard for him to steady his voice as he said, "Miss Dahlia, it's good to see your kind face again. It's been lonesome having the big house closed for so long and it's glad I am to have it opened."

Tears rolled down the wrinkled cheeks of the little old lady. This home-coming was hard, for, during the last two years Miss Ursula had been much changed, more of a loving sister and a comrade.

When they reached the house, Mrs. Sperry was on the veranda and Bertha, now a tall girl of eleven, was standing shyly at her mother's side.

The doors were wide open, and Nan, glancing in, saw that there were bowls of ferns and flowers in the hall and library. As she greeted Mrs. Sperry, she said softly, "It was very kind of you to do all this."

Then the girl assisted Miss Dahlia up the wide front stairs. The gardener's wife called after them "when you've laid off your wraps come down to the dining room. It's nearly noon and I thought you might be hungry after traveling so far."

"Thank you, Mrs. Sperry, we will," Nan replied, and tears sprang to her eyes as she thought how loyal these kind people were and with no hope of remuneration.

Later, while they were eating the appetizing luncheon which the gardener's wife was serving, Miss Dahlia asked, "Mrs. Sperry, will you see about hiring maids and a cook for us as soon as possible?"

The woman glanced at Nan questioningly and that girl hurried to say:

"Oh, Aunt Dahlia dear, please don't let's have any just yet. I do want to learn to keep house and the best way to learn, you know, is really to do it. Don't you think so, Mrs. Sperry?"

"Indeed I do, Miss Nan," that little woman replied with enthusiasm, "and I'll be right handy by, whenever you need help extra, for cleaning days and the like."

Miss Dahlia smiled. "Well dearie," she said, "you may try for a week or so, but at the end of that time, I'm pretty sure that you will be glad to hire a cook and at least one maid."

The next morning, when Miss Dahlia awakened, it was to see a smiling lassie in a pretty ruffled white apron approaching her bedside with a tray on which was a cup of steaming coffee and a covered plate of delicately browned toast.

"Top o' the morning to you, Aunt Dahlia," the girl laughingly called as she brought a wash cloth and towel and then a dainty lavender dressing jacket and cap. A few minutes later when the pleased little old lady was sitting up among comfortably placed pillows, Nan with arms akimbo, inquired, "Is there anything more ye'll be afther wantin' this mornin', Miss Barrington?"

"Oh, Nan darling," the little woman replied brightly, "I truly did think that I wouldn't be able to get on without Norah, but I believe that after all my new maid is going to prove a much handier young person. Have you breakfasted, my dear?"

"That I have, Aunt Dahlia, and my head is as full of delightful plans as a Christmas pudding is of plums, but first I wish to ask if I may have your permission to play the game just as I wish."

"Indeed you have it without the asking. Get all the amusement that you can get of the experiment, but, Nan dearie, don't you think that you would better reconsider and have at least one house maid?"

The girl shook her head and her dark eyes danced merrily as she again returned to Norah's brogue. "And is it discharging me, ye are, on the very fust day of me service wid ye? Arrah, and oi'll not be goin' till ye've given me a fair two weeks' triol."

Miss Dahlia smiled happily. What a comfort this gypsy girl was to her. Then suddenly the little woman realized that she had not thought of Nan as a gypsy for a long time. It did not seem possible that this loving and lovable girl could be the same little wild waif who had climbed out of an upper window nearly four years ago because she did not want to be civilized.

111

When the tray was ready to be carried away, the audacious maid stooped and kissed the smiling face of the little old lady as she inquired, "Will ye dress now, or will ye be staying' in bed for the mornin', Miss Dahlia?"

"I'd like to remain in bed, dearie, if you are sure that you don't need me to help you around the house. It was a long journey across the continent and now that we are really home it seems so nice to just rest and look out of the window at the garden and the sea."

"Good! I'm glad!" Nan exclaimed as she drew the downy quilt over the frail shoulders. "Perhaps you'll return to dreamland awhile. Now, don't forget that you have granted me permission to carry out my plans in my own sweet way."

When Nan was gone, the little old lady, resting luxuriously, wondered what her dear child might be planning, and then, truly weary, she again fell into a refreshing slumber.

Meanwhile Nan had donned her riding habit and, having visited the barn, she found her Binnie in fine trim. The small horse whinnied joyfully when he beheld his mistress, and Nan, putting her arms about him, caressed him lovingly. Two years before she had written Mrs. Sperry, telling her to permit the children to ride Binnie, and so the small horse had had many a merry canter and had not been lonely.

Saddling and mounting her mottled pony, Nan rode down the circling drive to the lodge house. She was about to carry out a plan, which was merely another way to economize and not let Miss Dahlia recognize it as such.

CHAPTER XXX.

NAN AS HOUSEKEEPER.

"Good morning, Mrs. Sperry," Nan called as she drew rein at the door of the lodge. "Could Bertha go up to the house and stay until I have cantered into town and back? Miss Dahlia is still in bed and I have a few purchases to make."

Then Nan told her new plan and the gardener's wife replied, "Bertha and Bobsy are in school. They take their lunch and stay all day and my husband works over at Baxters' now till mid-afternoon, so I'll take my basket of darning and go right up to be near Miss Dahlia if she should call."

"Thank you, Mrs. Sperry, I won't be gone long and you'll find my room just flooded with sunshine."

An hour later Nan returned and soon thereafter a delivery wagon left a bundle at the kitchen door. Mrs. Sperry declared that she could stay all the morning just as well as not.

Miss Dahlia did not awaken. Now and then Mrs. Sperry heard the tapping of a hammer from the ground floor where the kitchen and maid's dining room were and she wondered what Miss Dahlia would think of the new plan.

At about noon, Nan tiptoed upstairs and the gardener's wife looked up with a welcoming smile. "I'm on the last hole in the last stocking," she said softly. "I'm so glad to have them all done." Then she added, "Is the new plan finished?"

The girl nodded. "I do hope Aunt Dahlia will like it," she said.

"Nan, dearie," a sweet voice called from the next room, and Mrs. Sperry taking her basket of darned stockings, nodded goodbye and tiptoed away while the girl went to answer the call.

"I've had such a restful sleep, dear," the little old lady said, "and now I'll dress and help you prepare our lunch. Really, Nan, I shall enjoy being allowed to go into a kitchen again. You know when I was a girl it was considered both proper and fashionable for a young lady to learn how to cook that she might direct her servants intelligently, if for no other reason, and many times I've wished I might slip down, when the cook was away, and see if I could still make some of the things as my dear mother taught me, but Sister Ursula did not approve. She said one of the maids might see me and think that I was queer."

Nan laughed. "What fun we will have, Aunt Dahlia," she declared as she assisted the little old lady to dress, "for, if you will, I would like to have you teach me to cook as your mother taught you."

Then, when they were ready to go down stairs, Miss Dahlia said with almost girlish eagerness, "This afternoon we'll go up in the attic. There's a box somewhere up there which is filled with books, and in one of them my mother kept her tried recipes."

Nan led the way past the cold, formal dining room, with its polished table and high-backed carved chairs. The little old lay shuddered as she glanced in. "It will be hard to get used to having Sister Ursula's place always vacant," she said.

"I knew it would, dear Aunt Dahlia," the girl replied, as she put an arm about the little lady, "and that's why I have planned to have our dining room somewhere else."

They had reached the ground floor and the girl opened a door. Miss Dahlia glanced in and then she exclaimed with real pleasure, "Nan, how charmingly you have arranged this little room!"

It had formerly been the maids' dining room. It was on a level with the ground. The wide windows opened upon the garden, a lilac bush, close to the house was fragrant with bloom, and a mocking bird, somewhere near, was singing joyously. But it was the inside which had been transformed as though by magic. Nan had scrubbed the creamy walls and woodwork and had hung blue and white draperies at the sunny windows, while at one side stood a high long basket-box of drooping ferns. The table was daintily set with blue bird dishes which Nan had used in boarding school when she had a spread for her friends. There were only two chairs, and, since Miss

Ursula had never dined in this room, the loneliness of one gone could not be so keenly felt.

"Be seated, my lady," the merry girl said as she drew out the chair that faced the garden. "You are now to partake of the very first meal that your new cook has ever prepared." Miss Dahlia was delighted with the dainty luncheon. Nan chatted joyously, although whenever she was alone, she pondered deeply on how to solve the serious problem that was confronting them.

CHAPTER XXXI.

NAN'S PROBLEM.

That morning when Nan had been in the village of San Seritos, she deposited in the bank the money which Miss Ursula had left in her keeping. The interest from the few thousand dollars would be sufficient, the girl thought, to provide comforts and even some luxuries for Miss Dahlia, but the necessities Nan wished to earn, knowing that if they used the principal, it would soon be necessary to tell Miss Dahlia of the lost fortune, and the home which the little old lady so dearly loved, would have to be sold.

Before leaving Pine Crest Nan had talked the matter over with Mrs. Dorsey and that kindly woman had written a letter telling whoever might be interested that in her opinion Nan Barrington was competent to teach the younger children all of the required studies, as well as languages and the harp.

The girl was confident that she could obtain a position as governess but that would necessitate hiring a maid or leaving Miss Dahlia alone, and neither of these things did she wish to do.

A week had passed when one morning Nan sitting on the sunny veranda reading the paper chanced to see in the want column something which she thought that she would like to investigate.

Miss Dahlia was still asleep and Mrs. Sperry gladly took her sewing up to the big house while Nan rode away on Binnie.

She had not far to go, for a quarter of a mile down the coast highway was a group of picturesque bungalows about a small hotel called Miracielo. Here each summer wealthy folk from the inland country came and took up their abode. This year it chanced that there were many young children among the tourists, and Mrs. Welton, manager of the exclusive hotel, had advertised for someone who would both instruct and entertain the little guests.

Nan was admitted to Mrs. Welton's reception room and almost immediately a pleasant woman of refinement appeared and graciously welcomed the visitor. Nan explained her mission and showed the letter from Mrs. Dorsey.

"This is indeed interesting," Mrs. Welton exclaimed. "My niece, Daisy Wells, attends that school and in her letters she has often mentioned Nan Barrington." Then the kindly woman hesitated as though not quite certain that she ought to voice the thought that had come to her. Finally she said: "You will pardon me, I know, for mentioning a matter so personal, but I have always understood that your aunt possessed great wealth. Will she be willing that you entertain these little ones?"

Nan, after a moment's thought, decided to tell Mrs. Welton the whole truth and that good woman was much impressed in favor of the girl who was trying in every way to keep the frail Miss Dahlia Barrington from a knowledge of the loss.

"It would not be possible for me to come each day to Miracielo," Nan said, "but we have such a delightful rustic house in our garden; do you suppose, Mrs. Welton, that the children might come there each afternoon if I can persuade Aunt Dahlia to think favorably of my plan?"

"I do indeed," the pleased woman smilingly agreed. "That is the time when many of my guests desire to rest, and they would be glad to have the children away. If their mothers consent, I can send the little ones to you in our car every day."

Nan arose, her dark eyes glowing. "I thank you Mrs. Welton," she said, "and tomorrow I will let you know if I have won my aunt's consent to the plan."

That afternoon the gypsy girl broached the subject of the little class almost timidly, and her aunt said lovingly, "But, Nan, darling, don't you realize that all I have is also yours? You do not need to earn money."

"Dear Aunt Dahlia," the girl replied with sudden tears in her eyes, "I well know that whatever you have, you wish to share with me, but truly I would just love to try teaching for a short time."

"My Nan seems to wish to make many experiments," the little old lady said merrily. "Is not housekeeping enough?" Then, noting an expression of disappointment in the face of the girl, she added, "Bring your flock of children to our garden, if you wish dearie, I, too, will enjoy having them here."

And so, the very next afternoon a dozen boys and girls, the oldest not seven, appeared, and though, for a time, some of them seemed shy, Nan soon won their confidence and had them merrily romping on a velvety stretch of lawn which she had chosen for a playground. Then when they were weary, they went into the vine-covered rustic house, and, sitting about the long table, they played quiet games that were both instructive and amusing.

After receiving her first week's check, Nan visited the town and purchased books and materials that would assist her in teaching and entertaining her little "guests."

Happy times Miss Dahlia and Nan had in the long evenings as they sat in the cheerfully lighted library reading these books, and then they would try to weave a pattern from gaily colored wools or bright strips of paper according to the instructions. The next day that particular pattern would be the one that Nan would show the children how to make.

One afternoon Miss Dahlia wandered out to the rustic house during this rest period, and, sitting at one end of the table she assisted a darling five-year-old to make a paper mat of glowing colors.

"See, Miss Nan," the little fairy called joyously when the task was done, "see my pitty mat! May I take it home to show muvver?"

"Yes indeed, dearies, you may all take home whatever you make," their young teacher told them.

"I wish we could make doggies or elphunts," one small boy said. And that night Miss Dahlia and Nan hunted through the books for instructions on "elphunt" making, but failed to find them. Then Nan, not wishing to disappoint the little lad, brought forth scissors and cardboard and after many amusing failures, at last cut out a figure which Miss Dahlia laughingly assured the artist could be recognized as an "elphunt" at a single glance. They then cut out a dozen that the children might each have a pattern.

The little boy was delighted because his suggestion had been followed. Nan showed them how to make their card-board animals stand, and soon they had a long procession of rather queerly shaped "elphunts" and dogs all the way down the length of the table. The pleased children clapped their hands gleefully, and one little girl looked up with laughing eyes as she said: "Miss Nan, it's as nice as a party every day, isn't it?"

Sometimes the older girl, watching these children of the rich as they romped about on the velvety lawn, recalled another picture of the long ago. A group of dark-haired, dark-skinned, fox-like little creatures scrambling and rolling over each other as puppies do, but, when Nan had appeared, they had left their play and raced to meet her with outstretched arms.

How she would like to see them all again. Nan's life was happy but uneventful. The beautiful sunny, summery days passed and Nan's little class never wearied of the "Party-school."

Then all at once unexpected and surprising, events followed close, one after another.

CHAPTER XXXII.

SURPRISING THINGS HAPPEN.

It was Autumn once more. The children with their parents had returned to inland homes and the garden no longer echoed with their shouts and laughter.

Mrs. Welton had told Nan that the winter tourists from the snowy East would arrive in January and that she would re-engage her at that time if she cared to continue her little class, which the eager girl gladly consented to do. The remuneration had been excellent, and, during the intervening months, Nan planned keeping happily busy with sewing and home-making.

The garden was again glowing with yellow chrysanthemums as it had been on that long ago day when the gypsy girl and the little lad Tirol had first found the beach gate and the home which Nan had little dreamed was to be her own.

During the summer there had been many letters from Phyllis who was traveling abroad and from Robert Widdemere. Upon leaving the military academy, the lad's first desire had been to cross the continent at once, but, when he found many tasks waiting in his father's office, he believed that he ought not to start on a pleasure trip until these had been in some measure accomplished and it was November before he decided that he could start on the long planned journey. When he told his mother of his decision, she announced that she intended accompanying him and remaining during the winter at their San Seritos home.

This was a keen disappointment to the lad, who believed that his mother merely wished to try to prevent, if she could, his friendship with Nan Barrington, but Robert was too fine a lad to be discourteous, and so, on a blustery day, they left the East, and, in less than a week, they arrived in the garden village of San Seritos that was basking in the sunshine under a blue cloudless sky.

An hour later, Robert leaped over the little gate in the hedge and raced like a schoolboy across the wide velvety lawns of the Barrington estate.

He saw Nan and dear Miss Dahlia in the garden. At his joyous shout, they both looked up and beheld approaching them a tall lad who was jubilantly waving his cap.

"It's Robert Widdemere!" Nan said, and then, as he came up and greeted them, she added, "But only yesterday I had a letter from you and in it you said nothing about coming."

"I wanted to surprise you, Lady Red Bird," the lad exclaimed. "Isn't it grand and glorious, Nan, to be once more in this wonderful country. I wish we could start right now for a ride up the mountains."

"I couldn't go today," the gypsy girl laughingly told him, "for I have something baking in the oven and it cannot be left."

"I could tend to it," Miss Dahlia said, but Nan shook her head.

"It's a surprise for tomorrow," she merrily declared, "and I don't want even you, Aunt Dahlia, to know what it is."

Then turning happy eyes toward the lad, she said, "Think of it, Robert Widdemere, tomorrow will be Thanksgiving day and five years since you and I rode to the mountain top."

"Nan, comrade," the boy said eagerly, "let's take that ride again tomorrow, dressed gypsy-wise as we were before, shall we?"

"As you wish, Robert Widdemere," Nan laughingly replied. "Thanksgiving seems to be a fateful day for us."

A happy hour the young people spent together. Robert wished to hear all that happened and when Nan protested that she had written every least little thing, he declared that it had all been so interesting, it would bear repeating.

Suddenly the girl sprang up, holding out both hands as she exclaimed, "Robert, I shall have to ask you to come at some other time. I must look after that something which is baking for tomorrow." The lad caught the hands as he said, "Good-bye, then, I'll reappear at about ten."

CHAPTER XXXIII.

THE THANKSGIVING RIDE.

Thanksgiving morning dawned gloriously, and as Nan stood at her open window looking at the garden, all aglow, at the gleaming blue sky and sea, listening the while to the joyous song of a mocking bird in a pepper tree near, she thought how truly thankful she was that Fate had guided her to this wonderful place on that long ago Autumn day.

Miss Dahlia, who with the passing months had regained her strength, surprised the gypsy girl by appearing in the kitchen before that maiden had time to prepare the usual breakfast tray.

"Oh Nan darling," the little woman said as she held out both hands. "I am so thankful, so thankful today that I have you. Think how dreary even this beautiful world would be if I were alone in it."

The girl, with sudden tears in her eyes, kissed the little old lady lovingly as she replied, "I am the one who is most grateful. No mother could have been kinder to an own child than you have been to me." Then, brushing away a tear from the wrinkled cheeks, she laughingly added, "One might think that we were bemoaning some calamity instead of rejoicing because we have each other."

Merrily assuming Norah's dialect, to make the little old lady smile, Nan said, with arms akimbo, "Miss Dahlia, will ye be havin' some cream of wheat with thick yellow cream on it? Bobsy was just this minute after lavin' it."

And so it was a happy breakfast after all, and then, at ten o'clock Robert appeared dressed in gypsy fashion, and Nan, in her old costume of crimson and gold, the color of Autumn leaves in the sunshine, rode away with him on her pony Binnie.

The lad seemed to be exuberantly happy, as side by side, the two horses picked their way up the rough mountain road.

When at last they could ride no further, they dismounted and the lad turning to the girl said with tender solicitude, "Nan, every time that I glanced back without speaking, I caught a sad or troubled expression in your face. Won't you let me share whatever it is that causes you new anxiety?"

The girl flashed a radiant smile as she said self-rebukingly. "Truly, Robert, I have no real sorrow. But I am thoughtful, I must confess, and quite without willing it, I assure you. It is as though a thought comes to me from somewhere from someone else to me."

Then, knowing that she was not making herself clearly understood, she asked abruptly, "Robert, do you believe in mental telepathy."

The lad nodded. "I do indeed," he said. "Several of us cadets at school tried the thing out and the results were positively uncanny."

Then with a questioning glance at the dark girl, "Why, Nan, do you believe that you are receiving a telepathic communication?"

"Oh, I really don't know that I mean anything half as high sounding as all that. But what I do know is this. It doesn't matter where my thoughts may start, they always wind up with wondering where Manna Lou is. I am continually asking myself a question which I cannot answer.

"Will Manna Lou be remembering that I am now eighteen; indeed almost nineteen, and will she try to locate me that she may keep her long-ago-made promise to my mother?"

The lad looked into the dark eyes that were lifted to his. "Nan dear," he said very gently, "would you be greatly disappointed if this Manna Lou should find you and if the tale she has to reveal, should prove to be that you are not a gypsy girl at all." This was very like the question he had asked her in the long ago. Her answer had not changed.

Clearly she looked back at him. "Robert Widdemere," she said unhesitatingly, "all these years I have believed my mother to be a gypsy, and I have loved her as one. It would be very hard for me to change the picture, O the beautiful, beautiful picture I have in my heart of her!"

The lad, gazing into the glowing face could not resist saying, "Lady Red Bird, it is you who are beautiful."

But Nan, unlike many other girls, was not confused by so direct a compliment. She replied simply. "I hope I am like my mother."

The lad could wait no longer to tell the dream which had made his summer bright with hope. "Nan," he cried, "nearly four years ago we stood on this very rock looking down over the valley and I asked you to let me be your brother-comrade." Then, taking both of her hands, his voice trembling with earnestness, he continued. "And now, Nan, I have brought you here to this same spot to ask you to be my wife." Then, as she did not at once reply, Robert hurried on, "I know now that I loved you, even then, but we were too young to understand."

"Thank you, Robert Widdemere!" the girl replied. "I too care for you, but I could not marry you without your mother's consent."

And with that answer, the lad had to be content. After a moment's silence, Nan caught his arm and pointed to the highway far below them. "Robert," she said, "years ago as we stood here, we saw a strange car entering your grounds and in it was your mother who separated us for so long; and today, a strange car is entering the Barrington grounds. Who do you suppose has come to pay us a visit?"

"No one who can separate us again, Nan comrade," the lad said earnestly, "for no living creature can."

CHAPTER XXXIV.

A HAPPY SURPRISE.

The gardener's boy came on a run to take Binnie when Nan Barrington dismounted, and then the girl holding out her hand to her companion said, "Good-bye, Robert Widdemere. I would ask you to dine with us since it is Thanksgiving, but I know that it is right that you should be with your mother."

"But I'll be over by mid-afternoon, Nan," the lad earnestly replied, "and I shall ask you again the same question that I did this morning, but it will be with my mother's consent. Good-bye, dear, brave comrade."

As Nan turned into the house, she noticed a handsome car standing in the drive. For the moment, she had forgotten the visitor about whom they had wondered. Her heart was heavy with dread. What if it were someone who had come to tell Miss Dahlia about her lost fortune.

As she entered the wide hall, Miss Dahlia appeared in the library door and beckoned to her, and so the beautiful girl, dressed in crimson and gold, her cheeks flushed, her dark eyes glowing, accompanied her aunt, who seemed very much excited about something.

A tall, elegant gentleman was standing near the hearth.

"Monsieur Alecsandri," the little lady said, "this is the gypsy girl for whom you are searching. This is my Nan."

Unheeded the tears rolled down the wrinkled cheeks of Miss Dahlia as the stranger, with evident emotion, stepped forward, and held out both hands to the wondering girl, "And so you are Elenan, my dear sister's little daughter."

Nan looked, not only amazed, but distressed. "Oh, sir," she cried, "you are not a gypsy. My mother, wasn't she a gypsy after all?" Tears sprang to her dark eyes and the hand which Miss Dahlia held was trembling. The gentleman seemed surprised, but the little old lady explained, "Our Nan has been picturing her mother and father all these years as gypsies, and it is hard for her to change her thought about them."

The man advanced and took the girl's hands, and looking down at her earnestly, he said sincerely: "I am glad to find that you are not ashamed of your father's people, for he truly was a gypsy. He was Manna Lou's only brother. Now, if we may all be seated I will tell you the story. Your mother was born in a grey stone chateau overlooking the Danube River. Our father died when she was very young and our mother soon followed and so my orphaned little sister was left to my care. I thought that I was doing my best for her when I had her instructed in languages and arts, and then, just as she was budding into a charming and cultivated young womanhood, I had her betrothed to a descendant of Prince Couza.

"Other Rumanian young ladies envied my sister the social position which this alliance would give her, but Elenan begged me not to coerce her to marry a man whom she did not love. I was stern and unrelenting. All too late I learned that my sister loved Romola, a gypsy musician who was so rarely gifted that as a boy he had often played at the court for the king and queen. From them he had received many favors. He was placed in a monastery school to be educated, and, at his request, his younger sister Manna Lou was placed in a convent where she learned many things that other girls of her race never knew, but when they were old enough to do as they wished, gypsy fashion, they returned to the roaming life which was all that their ancestors had ever known.

"Often, Romola played the small harp he had fashioned in the court of Prince Couza, and it was there my sister met him. They loved each other dearly and were secretly married. I was away in another part of the country at the time, and, when I returned they had been gone for a fortnight. I searched everywhere for the gypsy band to which Romola belonged, but no one knew where it had gone."

The gentleman looked thoughtfully at the girl for a moment and then he continued: "I never fully abandoned the search, but, not knowing that they had come to America, I followed clues that led nowhere. I now know what happened. The son of Queen Mizella, fearing arrest for some misdeed, crossed the ocean to America and with them was my sister disguised as a gypsy.

"But on the voyage over your father Romola sickened and died. My poor sister was heart-broken and lived only long enough to give birth to a daughter, whom she left in the care of Manna Lou. She asked that kind gypsy woman to bring you up as one of her own band until you were eighteen. Then as your mother knew, you would inherit her share of the Alecsandri estate, and she asked Manna Lou, if it were possible when you reached that age to take you back to Rumania and to me. This, of course, the faithful gypsy woman could not do, but, with her band, she returned last summer and came to tell me the story. I had long grieved over my sister's loss not knowing to what desperation I had driven her, and so I at once set sail for America in search of her child. All that Manna Lou could tell me was that you had left the caravan near San Seritos, in California. When I arrived here and made inquiries, I learned that a gypsy girl had been adopted five years ago by Miss Barrington, and now, my quest is ended. I have found my sister's little girl."

Before Nan could reply. Miss Dahlia, glancing out of the window, exclaimed: "Nan, darling, Robert Widdemere is coming, and his mother is with him."

The girl sprang up. "Aunt Dahlia, Monsieur Alecsandri, if you will excuse me, I will admit Mrs. Widdemere and Robert. I would rather meet them alone." And so, before the lad had time to lift the heavy carved knocker, the door was opened by Nan. After a rather formal greeting, she led them into a small reception room.

It was hard for her to understand why Mrs. Widdemere had come, and she still felt dazed because of all she had so suddenly learned of her own dear mother.

"Won't you be seated?" the girl heard herself saying. Then to her surprise, Mrs. Widdemere, who had always so disliked her, took both of her hands, as she said "Miss Barrington, can you ever forgive me for the unkind way that I have treated you? My son has been telling me what a splendid, brave girl you are, and when I compare with you the one I wanted him to marry, how sadly she is found wanting. Only yesterday I received a letter telling me that she had left her mother, who is in deep sorrow, to accompany a party of gay friends on a pleasure trip to Europe. You cannot think how glad I am that my son did not heed my wishes in this matter."

Nan listened to this outburst, as one who could hardly comprehend, and for a moment she did not reply. Then she asked slowly, "Mrs. Widdemere, do I understand that you are now willing that your son should marry a gypsy girl?"

"Oh, Miss Barrington, Nan, what matters one's ancestry when the descendants of noble families are themselves so often ignoble? I have been a vain, foolish woman, but I know that true worth counts more than all else. If you can't forgive me, because I wish it, then try to forgive me for the sake of my son."

Tears gathered in the dark eyes of the girl, as she said, "Mrs. Widdemere, first I had a kind gypsy-aunt, Manna Lou, then two dear adopted aunts and no one could have been more loving than they, but now, at last, I am to have someone whom I can call 'mother.'"

"Thank you dear," the woman said, "I shall try to deserve so lovely and lovable a daughter. Robert, my son, you and I are much to be congratulated."

The lad, who had been standing quietly near, leaped forward and catching the hands of the girl whom he loved, he said joyously. "Nan, darling, let's have our wedding tomorrow out under the pepper tree."

The girl smiled happily, and then, suddenly remembering the waiting visitor, she said, "Mrs. Widdemere, I would like you and Robert to meet my uncle, who has just arrived from Rumania."

"A Rumanian gypsy," the lady was thinking, as she followed the girl. "That country is full of them."

A moment later, after greeting Miss Dahlia, she saw an elegant gentleman approaching and heard Nan saying, "Mrs. Widdemere, may I present my uncle, Monsieur Alecsandri?"

"Your uncle, Nan?" that lady exclaimed. "Surely this gentleman is not a gypsy."

"No, indeed, madame, I am not, but I am proud to be the uncle of this little gypsy girl." He placed his hand lovingly on the dark head. "Elenan is my sister's child, but her father was Romola, one of the handsomest and most talented of gypsies."

Then, that Robert and his mother might clearly understand, the story was retold from the beginning. The lad leaped forward, his hands outheld. "Oh Nan," he cried, "how glad you are that after all you are a real gypsy." Then he thought of something and turning toward the gentleman, he said in his frank, winning way. "Monsieur, Nan and I were to have been married soon. May we have your consent?"

The foreigner, although surprised and perhaps disappointed if he had hoped his sister's daughter would return with him, was most gracious. "If the very kind woman with whom I find our Elenan has given her permission, I also give mine."

There were sudden tears in the gentle eyes of the older woman. She had known of course, that some day these two would wed, but now, how could she live without Nan? Her hesitation was barely noticeable, then she said bravely. "I shall be proud, indeed, to have Robert Widdemere for a nephew."

Nan, noting the quivering lips, took her benefactress by the hand as she said brightly; "Oh, Aunt Dahlia, what do you think? I forgot our Thanksgiving dinner."

"But I didn't forget it!" that little lady quite herself again replied. "Mrs. Sperry has been in our kitchen all of the morning, and here she comes now to announce that dinner is ready for us and our three most welcomed guests."

Nan's cup of joy seemed full to the over-flowing but the day held for her still another happiness.

CHAPTER XXXV.
AN UNEXPECTED ARRIVAL.

On Thanksgiving afternoon Robert again said, "Nan, comrade, can't we be married tomorrow out under our very own pepper tree."

"Son," Mrs. Widdemere smilingly protested, "what an uncivilized suggestion for you to make."

"That's the very reason why I wish it," the lad replied. "Five years ago Nan and I met out under that tree and we both declared that we wanted to be uncivilized. I remember that I was pining to be a wild Indian or a pirate, but instead, we have both spent the intervening years in polishing our manners and intellects." Then turning to the girl, he pleaded, "Lady Red Bird, let me have my own way just this once, and then you may have your own way forever after."

Nan laughed happily. "But Robert," she said, "ought there not to be a trousseau before one is married?"

"Elenan." It was Monsieur Alecsandri who was speaking. "I was so confident I would find you, that I brought a trunk full of garments that were your dear mother's. It was the trousseau which I had provided for her when I betrothed her to a descendant of Prince Couza. The gowns are the loveliest that I could procure, but they were never worn."

"Oh, Uncle Basil." (He had asked the girl to call him by his Christian name.) "How glad I shall be to have them."

"But, Nan comrade," Robert repeated, "you have not yet said that I may plan our wedding and our trip away."

The girl looked at the lad who was seated on the lounge at her side and said brightly, "Robert, you plan it all and let it be a surprise for me."

Nan noticed that during the hour that followed Robert glanced at his watch and several times walked toward the window and gazed out toward the highway.

"Why are you so restless, son?" his mother had just inquired, when wheels were heard in the drive, and soon after the call of the heavy iron knocker resounded through the house. Robert half arose, but sank back to the lounge when he saw Mrs. Sperry going to the front door.

"Who can it be?" Little Miss Dahlia was quite in a flutter, but Nan had heard a voice inquiring if Miss Anne Barrington was at home?

With a cry of joy Nan sprang forward and held the newcomer in a long and loving embrace. "Phyllis, I can't believe that it is you!" she cried as she stood back to survey the pretty, laughing face of her dearest friend. "Why, it seems too much like a story book to be really true."

Then she led the newcomer into the library where she was gladly welcomed by all who knew her and introduced by Nan to "my uncle, Monsieur Alecsandri."

Phyllis, who never had believed that her room-mate was really a gypsy, took the arrival of an aristocratic uncle quite as a matter of course, and when they were all seated, Nan, still curious, exclaimed: "Do tell me how you happened to know that it was time to come to my wedding."

Phyllis looked up at Robert with a mischievous twinkle in her blue eyes. "Shall I tell?" she asked.

"I'll tell," that lad replied. "Last week I wired my fair cousin to board a train at once for the West if she wished to attend our wedding which I hoped would be solemnized on Thanksgiving day."

"Robert! How could you invite a guest to our wedding before you had asked me to marry you?" Nan laughingly declared.

"It was rather presumptuous," the lad confessed, "but all's well that ends well."

Monsieur Alecsandri accepted Miss Barrington's invitation to remain in her home, and Phyllis spent the night with Nan, for they had much to talk about. The latter maiden often fell to wondering what Robert's surprising plan was for their wedding.

CHAPTER XXXVI.

NAN'S TROUSSEAU.

The wedding day dawned gloriously. The two girls were up early and as soon as they were dressed, Nan drew her friend to the wide open window and they looked out at the garden, where masses of yellow chrysanthemums were glowing in the sunlight. Beyond, the wide silvery beach was glistening, and, over the gleaming blue water a flock of shining white sea gulls dipped and circled. Silently the two girls stood with arms about each other, and, in memory, Nan was again in the long ago. She was watching two children dressed in gypsy garb as they stood near the rushing, singing fountain. One was a dark, eager-eyed girl of thirteen, and the other was a mis-shapen, goblin-like boy of ten.

Tirol, dear little Tirol. How he had loved her, how he had clung to her! Tears gathered in the girl's eyes as she thought of the little fellow and she hoped that, somehow he might know what a happy day this was to be for his dear Sister Nan.

"Look yonder!" Phyllis laughingly exclaimed, "Here comes a mounted messenger at full speed."

"It's Bobsy, the gardener's son," Nan said. "He has been for an early ride on my Binnie."

The boy, chancing to see the two girls at the upper window, waved a letter, and, believing that he wished to give it to them, they went downstairs and out on the veranda.

The boy's freckled face was beaming. "Mr. Robert sent this over," he said jubilantly, "and he gave me a five dollar gold piece toward my new bicycle."

Then away the boy galloped to tell this astounding news to his mother, while Nan opened the letter and read:

"Good morning to you, Lady Red Bird. Can you believe it? This is our wedding day! I want to shout and sing, but I have much to do before that most wonderful of all hours, today at high noon.

"Since you promised that I might plan everything, I am asking my Nan to be dressed in gypsy fashion. Then your kinsfolk and my kinsfolk are to meet under the pepper tree as the bells of the old mission tell the hour of noon. Last night as I went through the hedge, I told our tree the great honor that was to befall it, and this morning the birds in it are singing a riotous song of joy, and I am sure that the pepper berries are redder than ever before.

"Then, at two o'clock will come the real surprise and the beginning of our joyous journey. Nan comrade, may I prove worthy of you!

"Your"ROBERT."

After breakfast Aunt Dahlia, Phyllis and Nan were wondering what the bride would wear for a wedding gown, when Monsieur Alecsandri returned from the station, whither he had gone at an early hour. A few moments later an expressman brought a trunk which was carried to Nan's room. Then her uncle Basil smilingly handed her a key as he said: "Elenan, do me the honor of wearing one of the gowns that were prepared for your mother's wedding."

Nan was indeed puzzled to know how she could please her uncle Basil, and yet keep her promise to Robert.

When the trunk was opened and the garments which it contained had been spread about on bed, lounge and chairs, Nan turned to the older lady, her dark eyes aglow as she said, "Aunt Dahlia, dear, did you ever see fabrics more beautiful?"

"This one is especially lovely," the little lady said as she smoothed the folds of a soft, white silk. "I wish you would try it on, dearie."

And then, when the girl stood arrayed in the gown, Phyllis exclaimed, "Nan, that surely was made for your wedding dress."

"But, Phyllis, you are forgetting Robert's request."

"No, I am not," the other maid laughingly replied. Then for a moment she looked about the room thoughtfully. Spying the gorgeous scarlet and gold shawl, which in the long ago Manna Lou had given the girl, she took it and threw one fringed corner over Nan's left shoulder, fastening it in front at the belt. Then, winding it about her waist, another point hung panelwise to the bottom of her skirt. The spangled yellow silk handkerchief was twined about the dark hair, and the picture reflected in the mirror was truly a beautiful one.

"Tres charmante!" Phyllis exclaimed jubilantly. "Now, let me see, there should be something old and something new, something borrowed and something blue. The dress is new, to us anyway; that gorgeous shawl is old. I'll loan you a handkerchief with a yellow and crimson border, and now, what shall you wear that is blue?"

Miss Dahlia slipped from the room to return a moment later with a velvet box which she handed to the girl she so loved. "My mother gave it to me when I was eighteen," the little lady said, "and I want to give it to my Nan on her wedding day."

The dark head and the fair bent eagerly over the box and when the cover was removed, the two girls uttered exclamations of joy.

"Oh, how lovely, lovely!" Phyllis cried as she lifted a sapphire necklace and clasped it about the throat of the happy Nan.

A busy morning was spent by the two girls, and, as it neared noon, Nan resplendently arrayed, looked up at Phyllis as she said, "I wonder where Aunt Dahlia is. She hasn't been here for half an hour past. Perhaps she is in her room. Wait dear, and I will see."

Miss Barrington's door was closed. Nan, after tapping, softly opened it. Miss Dahlia, with folded hands, was seated by the wide window gazing out at the sea and in her sweet grey eyes there was such a wistful loneliness. She looked up, as the girl entered, and smiled faintly, then her lips quivered and the tears came.

"Oh, Aunt Dahlia, darling! How selfish I have been!" Nan cried, as heedless of her white silk dress, she knelt by the little woman and put her arms lovingly about her. "I never thought! Perhaps you didn't want me to get married. But it isn't too late, Aunt Dahlia, if you do not wish it."

"Dear little girl," the old lady said tenderly, "of course I want you to be married. If I had searched the world over, I could not have chosen a lad whom I would like better. It is I who am selfish. I was fearing that Robert would take you away, and I don't want to lose my Nan."

"Lose me, Aunt Dahlia? Do you think that I would let you lose me? You are dearer to me than all the world, and where I go, you shall go, but we will always come back, won't we dearie, back to our garden-all-aglow where we have been so happy. Hark, the first stroke of the mission bells is telling that it is noon, and we must not be late at our very own wedding. Yes, Phyllis we are coming."

Monsieur Alecsandri was waiting for them in the library. Together they started along the flower bordered path toward the pepper tree, and Nan's wedding music was the joyous song of the birds.

CHAPTER XXXVII.
NAN'S WEDDING.

The ceremony was a simple one, but the solemnity, which Mrs. Widdemere feared would be absent, seemed to be enhanced by the peaceful beauty of the surroundings. All was hushed, not a bird sang nor a breeze stirred as reverently the two, arrayed as gypsies spoke the sacred words that made them man and wife. Then, when the rector from St. Martin's-by-the-Sea had kissed the bride and congratulated the radiant Robert, he departed, leaving the kinsfolk alone. Nan turned first of all toward the little old lady in the silvery grey gown, who was smiling through tears, and she said joyously, "Aunt Dahlia darling, instead of losing your gypsy girl you have gained a gypsy boy." Then going to Mrs. Widdemere, Nan kissed her affectionately and said very softly, "Mother." Then turning to Monsieur Alecsandri she asked gayly, "Uncle Basil, what do you think of your nephew? Is he not a good looking Romany rye?"

That stately gentleman shook hands with Robert as he replied: "In Rumania there is not one who can excel him in manliness, and I know that he will care for my dear sister's little girl as I would wish her cared for. I am indeed thankful, Elenan, that I arrived in time for your wedding. This afternoon I shall start on my homeward journey, hoping that in another year my niece and nephew, Mrs. Widdemere and Miss Barrington, will honor me with a long visit." Then he added earnestly, "Elenan, always remember that your mother's birthplace on the Danube River is as much your home as it is mine."

Then Mrs. Widdemere invited them through the gate in the hedge and, to their surprise, there on the other side, still under the spreading branches of the great old pepper tree, was a bare board table on which an appetizing lunch was spread gypsy-wise.

It was one o'clock when the feast was over. Robert, for a moment alone with Nan, said softly, "Little wife, put on that old gypsy dress now, for at two we will start on our trip away for a fortnight."

The girl looked up with a radiant smile as she said, "It shall be done, my husband."

The intervening hour was a busy one, for Monsieur Alecsandri took his departure, and then Nan, with the help of Phyllis, packed the few things she would need. Hearing a soft footfall back of her, the gypsy girl whirled about and caught Miss Barrington in her arms and held her in a long, loving embrace.

"I'm so happy, Aunt Dahlia, so happy," she said, "and just think what I would have missed from my life if you had not wanted to keep that wild little gothlin five years ago. I would never have had you to love, nor my best friend," the girl hesitated, and then with laughing eyes she added, "nor my husband."

"Hark!" Phyllis said. "I hear tinkling bells outside. What can it be?"

"It's a gypsy van," Nan cried joyfully, "and Robert is driving. That is the surprise and surely a delightful one."

Five minutes later these two joyful gypsies started away in a covered wagon, two horses in the lead, and Binnie, and Robert's saddle horse, Firefly, trailing behind. Phyllis was to remain with Aunt Dahlia during the fortnight and together they stood on the veranda waving until the gypsy van had turned into the highway. Nan looked up at the driver as she said happily, "Robert, this is a wonderful surprise." Then she added with sudden wistfulness, "I wish Manna Lou might have been at our wedding, but Uncle Basil promised to tell her all about it and give her my grateful love."

They were slowly ascending the mountain road, and, when they reached the ridge, Robert drew to one side and stopped. "Nan comrade," he said, "I want to climb to the top, for, somehow, it seems as though that peak must be our shrine for thanksgiving."

Then, when they reached the boulder where they had stood twice before, the lad took both of the girl's hands and looking into the dark glowing eyes, he said, "Elenan may be a fine Rumanian lady, if she wishes, but the comrade whom I love and always shall love is my dear, brave little wife, Gypsy Nan."

Then together, hand in hand, they went down the trail and soon the tinkling of bells was heard as the gypsy van slowly crossed over the ridge and down another mountain road, where, at sunset, these two would make camp in a picturesque canyon called Happy Valley.

Milton Keynes UK
Ingram Content Group UK Ltd.
UKHW010728200923
429044UK00004B/172